# The Devil's Due

## Charles J. Grimes

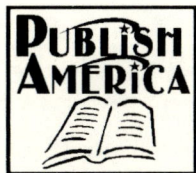

PublishAmerica
Baltimore

First printing

ISBN: 1-59129-845-8
PUBLISHED BY PUBLISHAMERICA BOOK
PUBLISHERS
www.publishamerica.com
Baltimore

Printed in the United States of America

*This is dedicated to my wife Jenni
and my children Heather, Aaron, Megan and Kelsey.
Thanks for putting up with the "cowboy" in me.*

# ACKNOWLEDGMENTS

I want to thank Becky Stewart and
Joyce Lovins for years of encouragement.

Carla Kemper, my computer guru.

Sarah Wilz my photographer.

Eugene Stewart agent/attorney.

Miss Nancy Hamilton – who taught me to write a complete
sentence.

My Buddies: Uncle Gil Grimes, Orville Bever and
Jim Siebert. "Thanks for the Mayberry Moments!"

My Mother, A Survivor

My stepfather, George Jenks he was there when we most
needed him.

To the memory of James and Margaret Jackson, my
surrogate parents.

My late Uncle Bob Grimes

# INTRODUCTION

This story alludes to the mysterious history of the Melungeon peoples. Melungeons are a people of hidden or 'lost' past. In previous centuries it was necessary to conceal one's past because of racial overtones that lead to discrimination and abuse.

Melungeons are a mixed blood of people that usually find their stories going back to the Appalachian areas in the early years of our country's founding. Many peoples of various races [native American, Anglo Saxon, Hispanic, African, etc.] met in the wilderness and for various reasons, 'love' being the most prevalent, intermarried.

Due to laws that discriminated against those of mixed blood from owning land, having various other legal rights, and general miscegenation restrictions, many, of Melungeon background, destroyed documents, photos, paintings, and other evidence of their heritage.

It is only in recent times that these proud, but hidden histories are being made known. People with the various physical features, i.e. the knot at the base of the skull, pigmentation differences in skin, high cheekbones, dark hair, are communicating and joining together in Melungeon organizations. They attempt to find the 'missing links' in their past through contact with 'like' peoples.

This story is not intended to reflect negatively on the Melungeon people. They are an integral part of our American History, albeit, a mysterious and often lost segment. They experienced great luck, both good and bad, though not all, of their own making…. I know, for I am Melungeon.

Charles J. Grimes  6/1/02

He would've been in his late twenties at the peak of the Revolutionary War.

I pondered the thought, as I stood over the old veteran's grave. "Died 1832, age 83 yrs.' served, Col. Latimer's Lexington Alarm Company, with valor." was written on the stone. A veteran's marker, was also stuck into the sod beside the stone. A strange feeling of recognition came over me. I continued my evening walk.

Days later, I still couldn't get the thought out of my head, that this person, buried in a lonely old graveyard in southern Indiana, was a long way from his beginnings. He'd been a man from the East, who'd seen the British soldiers, eye to eye. He was a connection to our historic past. Days on end, while my students worked and struggled over Jr. High History, I would gaze from my second floor room out over the old cemetery across the street and think of the man. Who was he? What wonders did he experience? How did he end up here?.... Then he spoke to me.

# Chapter 1

It was a mild September evening, the leaves were turning color and beginning to fall. Some where, off in the town, someone was violating the 'no-burning ordinance,' but the light smell of burnt leaves was pleasing to the nostrils. I was on my evening walk. Every day after school, I had my ritual of feeding my cattle and dogs, checking fence, and 'doodling' around the barn. Before supper, I'd walk from home (which sets on a hill north of but adjoining the town limits) through the woods and the town, thereby getting a couple miles of much needed exercise, both mental and physical.

Each evening I found myself going by the graveyard, inspecting different stones, and reading the inscriptions on them. "Aged 16 yrs, Drowned in the East fork of the Whitewater river, 1823," so many sad stories of young lives snuffed out by misfortune and illness. It was all very interesting to an amateur historian like me. I found myself ending each visit at the old veteran's grave, just sitting in the cool grass, watching the sunset, and thinking.

I tried to envision what type person 'he' had been. He'd served in the Revolutionary war in the northeast, and then traveled west, into the primitive northwest territory and settling, and eventually dying, in this lonely place.

Quite suddenly, I felt a surreal uplifting of my inner soul, my senses were tingling. I was scared and exhilarated at the same time. The short neck hairs stood ridged! A mist, or fog, surrounded me, as it cleared… I saw him…. sitting across the grave, in an old wooden rocker.

He was ancient and grizzled, with long white hair, that hung limply below his shoulders. His wrinkled, dark face was clean shaven. He wore homespun garments, a weathered, but clean shirt, of off-white cotton. He had on brown cotton trousers, held up with a wide black belt. He boots were of worn brown leather.

"Surprise you son?" he smiled and asked.

I was dumbstruck.

He spoke again, "Frankly speaking, I was surprised to 'feel' someone with so much concern and emotion. It is a rarity, but I knowed you was the one. Yessir, you be the one."

"The one?" I managed to mumble.

"Yessir, you be the one to tell my story, and the stories of the rest of us saints and sinners here in our final rests."

I sat in a dazed stupor. "What is happening?" I asked myself," Am I having a stroke? Have I lost my mind?" I was forty-eight years old, a point in life where the unexpected bodily mishaps become the expected." Perhaps I'll just sit a spell and this will pass."

"No, it won't go away." The old man quietly chuckled through toothless lips. "You're the one. You care, you feel, and we both want you to know our story. People nowadays want to makeup tales of the past. They have their own beliefs based on what someone wrote down. Someone, who was never there to see it happen!" He became animated, I jumped! "Easy son," he cautioned, "I get a bit worked up when I get to thinking. I've had a lot of time to do that, ye know!"

I nodded in silent agreement, not knowing whether I would offend or flatter this 'haint', by commenting on his "thinking years." He leaned forward and the old chair creaked.

"Son, ye were sent here for a reason. Just reach out real slow-like, and touch my sleeve."

I slowly rolled up from my sitting position to my knees, reached across the grave, and easily laid my hand on the tattered sleeve of the well-worn shirt. It was soft and comforting. A glow of light came over the scene. We simultaneously rose to our feet. The area around us was changed. The Middle school across the street, and all the homes were gone, replaced by trees and brush. I released my touch on his sleeve and slowly turned. There were only a few homes scattered here and there among the trees. Most of them were log, with an occasional clapboard home. They were of the early frontier style, but appeared newly built. Across the cemetery, which now consisted of fewer gravestones, was a small gathering by an open grave. Four people were lowering a pine casket into the grave. There was not a mourner, or preacher in site.

"What's going on?" I asked. Was this a dream, a delusion, depression?

We seemed to glide across the grass. Slowly the strange scene came into clearer focus.

I felt as old Scrooge must have felt."Must've been something I ate. a bit of undone potato, or overcooked stew."

"You're fine young fella," he gently stated, "Just take it all in very slowly, watch and listen."

The four men finished lowering the casket and immediately

began shoveling dirt into the hole. Grumbles and curses came from their lips as they quickly finished the task. As the last shovel of dirt was tossed on the grave, two men walked from a wooded area south of the cemetery, carrying a large boulder. They shuffled to head of the freshly-mounded earth and let the stone drop, with a resounding thud! The six men, all dressed in homespun clothing of another era, stood silently.

I found myself and the old man being drawn closer until we were within a few feet of the somber scene, seemingly unnoticed. I realized the we were at a spot in the cemetery where just a few days before, I had discovered a solitary grave, located several feet away from the rest. It was marked with a small white military veterans' stone and read, "Lester Goins, Company A, U.S. Col. Infantry." I'd briefly pondered the plight of a black man, buried in this all-white cemetery, in this all-white community. Isaac and I stood quietly as one of the men in the group before us, spoke.

"He really wasn't a bad-seeming feller." A young man in his early twenties, sadly stated.

"Ah hell, Joel, ye knowed what they said about him all along." Said an older fellow with rough features, and a full beard that gently waved in the misty breeze. "He wuz trouble from day one, just by being colored. He never did quite fit into our community, and in the end he showed his true colors!"

Soured chuckles of agreement and nods came from the others.

A big man in his mature years, and apparently the leader of the group spat a wad of dark brown tobacco juice at the foot of the grave and said, "It's over boys. Whatever he was before he came here, he ended up a murdering, raping bastard who got what he deserved! Let him go to the devil with that noose around his gullet. Let's go have a drink." They all nodded in agreement, turned, and trudged slowly away into the mist towards the small settlement to the west. We stood alone beside the fresh grave.

I was surprised to see the old man begin to walk slowly back towards his gravesite. I hurried after him, and cried, "Wait, what was that all about? I need some explanation. What's going on?"

The old fellow had tears in his eyes as he turned to me and said, "Too many memories son. I need to rest and ponder." He went to his rocker and sat. He began to rock quietly and rubbed a weathered hand over his white haired-head.

I knelt before him and pleaded. "Tell me, please! I need an explanation. Is this a dream?"

He gave me a withered look, as the tears dripped from his checks. I extended my arm, but the tears disappeared before they reached my hand. I withdrew and sat quietly. He wiped his eyes with his sleeve, and leaned forward in the chair. "You're the one," He repeated several times, "You have to help us."

"Okay," I gently stated, "but I have to know. I have to have the facts. Right now, I don't even know for sure who I am!"

"Oh your fine," he calmly said. "You'll be fine, but there's a load that I intend to burden you with, and then you'll have the obligation to deal with it and set things right."

I sat quietly in wonder. A short time ago, I'd been a respected middle school teacher of social studies in my hometown. I was considered by many to be a level headed community leader. Now, I was sitting in a graveyard, in some kind of time warp, and talking with a ghost from the past. I was seeing even stranger things, and agreeing to participate in even stranger events!

He spoke quietly as he dried his eyes on his tattered sleeve. "You see son, things aren't what they seem to be. That poor boy they just planted over there, and I, share a common thread. We need to be released. Our penance is to endure until the truth is known to all. Until then, we lay here in our silent tombs as the world goes by. Others travel on, to their spiritual homes, we lay in limbo, a common hell, where there is no peace, only sorrow and remorse." He quietly leaned back in the old chair and began to slowly rock. The years of torment, lined his weathered features.

"We dealt with the Devil, unwittingly. We unknowingly committed horrendous sins. We are innocents, guilty of ignorance, greed, and lust. All of our earthly good deeds cannot overcome our transgressions. We need others to know, so they may not follow in our footsteps. Only then, can our souls be released for final judgement."

I cleared my throat and cautiously ask, "If your transgressions were so great, do you really wish to face that final judgement?"

A glimmer of light appeared in his eyes, as he smiled and said. "Son, as I mentioned, we meant well, but did wrong. There can be no judgement so harsh as the blackness we have been condemned to for the ages. You have been sent to us as a ray of hope for salvation. Don't doubt, or fail us."

"I'll try my best." I timidly stated, as I studied his features. They were agonized and appealed for help. There was hope, desperation, anger and fear, all entwined in one face. His head reclined to the high-backed rocker. His eyes closed. He was quiet. He appeared to be in deep thought or sleep.

After a short period, I finally asked, "Are you alright?"

"Hell no, I'm not allright!" He blurted, " I'm trying to figure out how in tarnation I can lay all this before you in terms so's you'll be understanding! I'm contemplating my past, my future, and trying to align events so's I can figure out how I'll explain this to a mortal, who's just been dropped into this mess!"

By this time I was a bit frazzled. I gave a flippant reply. "Oh, okay, just take your time, you old ghost!"

"Don't get uppity with me, boy!" he shouted, " I've seen better come and better go, but you're all we got, so we'll make do which what we have!"

"Well," I replied. " I suppose you'll see 'better' the next time around. I may as well move on!"

"Don't move!" he commanded. "We need you. You've been sent to be our mediator…..Please."

"Who sent me?"

"Don't ask, just believe. You took my sleeve and walked across the graveyard. You've talked with me. You see me. Don't you believe me?" he pleaded.

"Yes, I guess so. I doubt this is like a dream, or nightmare, but I have a family and a home. I have classes to prepare for…."

"I know," he cut in, " You'll go on with your life, but you've found time to come here real regular-like, and if you'll just continue, I can work with you and fill you in as we go, and possibly you can be of help."

"Okay, okay," I said, " but perhaps I'd better go and think on this, and return tomorrow. By the way who was that fellow just buried over there, and why was he hanged?"

He sadly smiled and said, " As you said…tomorrow." He was gone as suddenly as he'd appeared. The fog disintegrated. It was twilight. The school and homes were all back in their places. Only a few moments had passed in real time. I remained seated in the cool grass, then I arose, and slowly made my way home.

My home sits in the middle of thirty acres on a hill, overlooking the town of Brookville. It is a modest chalet, with upper and lower decks, and a great room, facing the town (to the south) with sixteen huge panes of glass for a wall. The view is beautiful in all seasons. I can seen the entire valley, and down into the main street of the town. The church spires, commercial buildings, and the courthouse steeple, all give me many moments of peace and comfort. I enjoy spending the leisure hours daydreaming, in my favorite armchair. Tonight would be different.

My wife of many years, Jenni, is an elementary teacher at the local school. She was preparing the evening meal as I entered the kitchen. " How was your walk?" she asked.

"Fine," I mumbled, as I flopped down at the counter. I sat in silence, staring at the evening paper.

"You okay?" she ask, "You seem upset."

"Just reading the paper, why?" I absently answered.

She looked at me questioningly, "Well, the paper is upside down. Kinda challenging isn't it?"

"No, I'm fine." I quickly righted the error. " Been exploring the cemetery again. Some interesting people buried there."

"Oh yes!" she said, "I took my third graders on a field trip there last year. We made etchings of some of the more interesting headstones, and read the lettering on them. We may go back and do it again next spring."

"No!" I blurted, "I mean, the administration may feel it's a bit redundant to go to the same place so often."

"Well too bad! There's alot of our history there, and the kids really enjoy the hands-on experiences. They enjoyed making the etchings."

I was in a panic, "Well, everything is not as it seems!" I immediately regretted the outburst. She looked at me as if I just 'farted' in church.

"Are you sure you are okay. What you're saying doesn't

make much sense. What's the matter….afraid of ghosts?"

I laughed, a bit too loud. " Oh no, I'm just tired. Was a rough day at school. After supper, I intend to relax on the deck and turn in early."

Later, as the stars filled the sky on the cool autumn night, I rocked in my chair on the deck, smoked my favorite pipe, and pondered the day's events."Am I going crazy? Is this one of those Sixties' Acid-flashbacks, I'd heard happened to some of my friends? I'd missed out on Vietnam (high lottery draft number), so it wasn't 'Agent Orange.' Must be a slight aging stroke, or something. Think I'll skip the cemetery for a few days." I sat late into the night, pondering my dilemma. I found no answers, only more questions.

# Chapter 2

The next week, my evening walks were confined to the west of town, along the railroad tracks. I still was very concerned about the visitation (as I'd come to refer to it), and came to the conclusion that illusion or not, I had to return.

It was a warm and sunny autumn Saturday. I'd finished my chores of cattle feeding and barn cleaning. (I like to keep five or six head of young cattle on hand, as lawn mowers and mobile 'field fertilizers'). I had decided to revisit the cemetery in the full light of day.

A cool breeze rattled the leaves of the oaks and maples that lined the streets of the town. As I walked closer to the graveyard, I was filled with trepidation, but was pleased to see that all seemed "normal." I timidly entered, and strolled passed the old veteran's grave. Nothing. I walked on past the ancient stones, occasionally stopping to read and epitaph and note the dates. Soon I was near the south end of the cemetery overlooking the valley. I stood quietly in the autumn light, gazing out over the tranquil scene. "What a sight it must have been 200 years ago!" I thought.

"De old man said you'd be back." Someone behind me said.

My heart lurched at the sound of the voice! It was a young voice, with a thick syrupy sound. I slowly turned, and saw him!

He sat on the freshly mounded grave, where I witnessed the burial a few days ago. He was the 'colored' infantry soldier. He wore homespun cotton clothing of indiscriminate color (a greenish-brown). There were patches at the knees and elbows. He had no shoes. His skin was of light brown in color. He had a handsomely-pleasant face with high cheekbones, and very dark eyes. He nose was thin, his grin was full, with pearly white teeth. His short hair was tightly curled and coal-black. Most striking of all, was the rope that was knotted around his neck, the loose end, hanging down in front of his shirt. His neck had burn marks from the rope, and was slightly elongated, giving his head a crooked appearance, atop his shoulders. He seemed content and relaxed, but appeared in dire need of a chiropractor.

He sat quietly. I took full measure of him. I finally gathered my wits enough to say, with a false calmness, "You're him."

He let forth a deep chuckle and said, " It's me brother." His smile was one of warmth and friendliness. "Yessir, I'm de soul you here to see today. I 'been wiatin' quite a bit. Old man says you'd come back in you own time, to help out."

I sighed and spread my arms out at my sides, "Well I'm here, but I don't yet know what help I can be." I sat down at the opposite end of the grave. We stared into each others eyes.

"De old man didn't tell you nuttin' huh?" he smiled.

"No, I only know of your sad entombment, and that you were hanged for something. Other than that, only some mumblings about the two of you sharing a common bond or penance."

He chuckled, "De old man, he allus gotta talk in circles. Take him all day to splain what he had fo breakfast! Well, I'll just give you de basics and de old man'll fill you in wid his version later, I'm sure."

"Well," I thought, as I pinched my arm to see if this was real, "We're finally getting somewhere. But how will I ever explain this to anyone. People will think I'm crazy. Looks like counseling for me!"

"No, no," he laughingly said, " You gonna be fine. You knows how to handles things better than you think. Don' worry bout nuffin'."

"My God!" I thought, " He can read my mind! I' better just shut up an concentrate."

"An' dat's de truth!" he said, as he smiled again and stretched. The vertebrae in his crooked neck popped loudly. "Yeouch!" he cried. "I hope when dis is settled dat my neck comes back around. 'Been killin' me for over a hunnert years!"…Ghost humor?

I was again getting exasperated with this drawn-out display. "Well, either we are going to get on with this story or I'll be on my way! You fellows sure seem to like to drag things along. Guess you've nothing better to do!"

He jumped to his feet, "You want it white boy? You'll get it! Take my hand!" he commanded as he reached out to me, "Go on, grab aholt, real tight.

De color, it won't come off ye know." He chuckled at his joke.

The heavily veined arm extended to a callused hand, a hand that had seen years of hard work and toil. As I took hold, his grip became firm, but not painful. I was afraid, but felt a peaceful inner strength come through my arm, into my inner depths. A fog descended around us. We were back again in time, to a place of nearly one hundred and fifty years before. The smell of woodsmoke drifted across my nostrils. The sounds of distant horses hooves on dirt roads played in my ears. There was a peaceful calm all around.

He spoke quietly, " This is where it happened, 1868. The old man 'been gone nearly thirty years." A tear came to his eye. "I surely meant well, never wanted to do bad, but seems trouble always found me. Warn't good times to be a black man in dis here country. Oh, I's accepted, dat is… tolerated, such as I was, but it was lonely."

I sat in silence. Content to listen and allow his tortured soul remember.

After a brief pause, wiping a ragged sleeve across his eyes, he continued. "Was borned in ' 29 up in Indianapolis town. My mother was de only one 'round fo family. She was a dark-skinned gypsy woman, de tells me. She did voodoo and magic. Folks's real scared of her. One day, when I's just off de tit, she up a leaves me wif some of our peoples, and heads off up to de north. I's a burden to de family dat raised me, but dey say des glad to see her go. She wore flashy colored clothes. She had long black hair an wore lots of jewelry, big golden-hooped earrings. Dey says she was a beautiful woman wif wild ways. She scared nearly ever body 'round including white folks.They'd all call on her in times of need, fo medicines, potions, an "special needs." A poor sharecropper family took me in an' said I's de own, but took care not to show me off much in de area. I tried to behave, do chores, an work hard, but seemed trouble always find me. I got into several little scrapes but nothin' serious, til de day at de river.

"De children, both black an white, played together along de banks of de river that ran through the area. One day when I's bout twelve we all decided it would be good to have a swim. Well, we all stripped down an jumped in. Had a grand old time asplashin and hollerin'.

I decided to get out o' the water, des two white girls wuz astandin by our clothes an' giggln' and laughin. Des abit older than me, an dey's appointin at me an' laughin. Couple of the other boys ran off naked into the brush an hid. I wanted my clothes. One girl grabbed the clothes, an' she began to run. I ran after her into the brush. She was yellin' and giggling as she ran through the thicket. As she jumped a log, a vine caught her foot she fell, an' didn't move. I ran up to her. Her neck was bent real bad, an' her head was twisted. Must've broke it in the fall. I real quick, grabbed at the clothes an' was puttin' them on, when the other girl runned up at started screamin, "You killed her! You stupid darkie! You tried to pull her dress, an tripped her! They'll hang you for this!"

"Well, I's plenty scared an' worked up. She ran one way, an' I ran the other. Seemed I never stopped a-running. I hid out fo abit an' moved on. Was a big search party, but I's able to keep ahead of them. Lived by my wits an' hid out. Sometimes I'd steal, or find food in strange places. I'd be travellin' an' find bread or meat, as if it was left for me.

I slept in barns an' by de riverbanks. Travelled to de north an' didn't stop for many days. I finally arrived at Chicago city. Was a 'wonnerful' place to get lost in de crowd.

I found work in the town an' for farmers in the area. The time went by quickly. I grew up to be a strong young man. Learned to use my strength an' wits to get by. I always wondered about de happinins' back home. Wanted to find out about my people's. I began to work my way back south, an' ended up north of Indy. I used a different name. Was born Moses Brown, but changed to Lester Goins. I was in my twenties, an' people only new me as 'Lester', a refugee from the south.

"I'd learned how to get by during those youthful years in the north. Had to scramble for a meal and shelter, but made due. It helped when I returned to Indy, 'cause I had to still be 'on the slye', always worried if somebody'd recognize me. Never happened. Indy was a growing city, an' war fever was in the air. There was 'sussech' talk in the south, an' people in the north weren't goin' tolerate it."

"There was anti-slavery protests, an' the underground railroad was doin' a good business bringin' poor souls to the north and freedom. Was an excitin' time. I found work with the railroad asettin' rails an' ties. Was hard, but I got paid real regular. Was a busy time in our country!"

"Then bout '61 fighten' broke out in the south. Them dam Rebs started up sumpin' they couldn't handle. Was a callout for troops all over the north. Being of color, I figured they's nothin for me. I kept working at my job an' de months rolled by. No coloreds were wanted at de 'fust' of de war.Den, a fellow at the yards tells me 'bout a colored unit being set up at camp Morton. Couple of us boys headed over to the camp one mornin an' ask about joinin' up. Dis young white officer overheard us. He slapped me on the back an' said "Gentlemen you are now in the United States Army!" He gave us a big speech 'bout patriotism an' all dat bullshit. We just wanted out of town! We's in the army!" I signed in as Lester Goins (my new and forever name) an' was assigned to Company A, colored infantry.

"It was a good life at camp. We got up early an' practiced marchin' 'round. We got to fire guns abit. Wore fancy new uniforms that was too hot, but got plenty of food. Sho' was easier than workin' the railroad!"

"After 'bout thee weeks, we's told to pack our gear and git ready to ship out. Next thing I knowed, we's loaded into cattle cars an' on the way to Cincinnati, Ohio! Was a nice trip, jes' sittin on the straw an' watchin the countryside pass by through the open doors. Then we stopped in Brookville.

"I had a strange feelin' ' bout the place. Was a pretty little town, 'bout fourty miles from Cincy. I wanted to get off and look around. The officers told us to stay by our car and not to stray. Was a crowd of white people gathered at the depot, 'bout three cars up from us. I guess we was a real curiosity to them, being black and in army uniforms an' all."

Directly we' loaded back onto the cars an' started to pull away. Was then I saw her….., the prettiest dark skinned girl I'd ever seen. Her face stood out like a beacon in the white crowd. She seemed to be looking right through me!

She smiled an' waved. I smiled back an' waved and poof! She was gone. We was rollin' down the tracks out of view. What a sight she was! Told myself that I'd never forget her." He shook his head, and with a sorrowful look at me said, "Lord, how little did I know. Wish I'd never seen her!" He sat quietly for abit.

'What about her?" I asked.

"No, not yet." he stated, " I'm getting ahead of myself. Jus' let me go on with the story. I nodded and sat back. He gathered himself and continued.

"We didn't arrive in Cincy, 'til very late in the night. Had a mishap on the way. Seems some of the white officers in the front car was nip'n on a jug of corn whiskey all afternoon. A couple of' em stepped out onto the catwalk between cars to piss, when one slipped an' fell under the train. Lordy! His carcass was tore up an' spread out under the back four cars! Once they got the train stopped, guess who got the job of cleanin' him up?"

We unloaded and stripped off our tops, an' started pullin uniform an' body parts out from the wheels. Wasn't a whole lot left, but they put him into a gunnysack an' told us to go across the tracks to a nearby stream to wash up. Was nice by the stream. I was thirsty an' drank several mouthfuls of the cool water before I heard a fellow up a ways yellin' 'bout a dead cow in the water, an' tellin' us not to drink it. Too late! Oh well, It tasted okay.

"Like I said, we arrived abit late an' it was raining. We's marched down by the slaughter yards an' told to pitch our tents. I had a cold chill in my bones but paid no mind. The smell from all those cows an' hogs was enough to take your mind off anything."

"The next morning, I was up 'afore revalee a vomitin' an' had terrible loose bowels. They sent me to a big tent with other sick fellows. Thought I was gonna die! After several days I was able to get up an' move around, but they told me my company had moved on to the east. A white officer came by a said I's bein' mustered out of the army as 'unfit for duty'!

"I couldn't believe it. Felt fine, but the man said I's 'susceptible to fevers', whatever that means, an' they didn't want me to infect the others! Well I really didn't care bout missin' out of gettin all shot up in battles, but I's sad about leavin all my new friends. I's taken to the quartermaster's tent given my due pay an' signed my release papers. Was a sad day when I walked away from that place. No home, no friends, no army! He was quiet.

"What did you do then?" I asked.

"Well," he said, " I just went out an hung myself!" he gave the loose end of the noose on his neck a pull and held it above his head.

My eyes bulged! " You did what?"

"No,no" he laughed, "I jus' couldn't resist a little 'black' humor." He laughed loudly. He was cracking himself up! I smirked and scowled, miffed at my gullibility and his sick humor " I'm sorry," he finally said, " haven't had alot to joke about these last few years. You deserve better."

"It's okay," I said, " You caught me by surprise. I'm alright with it." We sat quietly for a few moments and then he began again.

"Well, I's down an' out again. Had to find work at the slaughterhouses. Worked the pens. Nasty job, it was! I had to drive stock to the killin' floor. Those old boars a gruntin' an' frothen', an' tryin' to rip you with dey tusks. Old bulls tryin' to run you over. My only defense was a wooden club an' quick moves. I gots the scars on my legs an' gut to prove it. The noise from the killen floors was bad. The screams an' bellows of those beasts goin' to dey deaths, an' in they death throes, still ring in my ears. The smell was even worse. Couldn't get it out of my clothes an' hair, even after a bath in the river." He sighed and slowly shook his head at the memory.

"I got along okay, worked hard an' got paid. Had a reputation as a fair hand. Lived in a shack with a couple other fellows, down by the river, not too far from the pens. We partied away our free times, which wasn't many, an' got through the winter that way. I still often wondered 'bout that pretty girl over in Indiana. Thought 'bout her specially when I's with the ladies. We'd visit the houses along the waterfront sometimes. There was plenty of women ready an willin' for a price.

One spring day I's roundin' up sows an' headin' them for the auction arena, when the straw boss came by an' hollered for me to come out of the pens. Said he heard I's knowledgeable 'bout Indiana an' he needed a man to drive some young heifers up a ways to the Brookville area. A wealthy farmer just east of the town had bought thirty head, an' needed them brought up. The boss said, he thought I's a dependable hand, an' since we's short of regular drovers, the war an' all, he wanted to send me an' a couple fellows up with the cattle. Said I'd get my regular

27

wage an' a old hoss. Said he'd sneak me an old revolver just for protection against thieves. Was illegal to give a black man a gun but, was to be between us. I accepted on the spot.

The next day me an' the two fellows I roomed with, was saddled up an' headed those cows for Indiana. Was a beautiful morning, as we headed up old Brookville road. The road went north and along the Whitewater river, an' later along the canal, all the way to Brookville. Was a pleasant an' uneventful two-day trip. We rested the stock often, an' camped along the river that first night. We took turns stayin' up the stand watch. When my turn came 'bout three o'clock. I found Jess, the second shift fellow, asleep by a tree. Kicked him hard in the ribs for neglectin' his duty. "Hey!" he shouted, "What the 'sam hill' the matter?"

I told him, "Boy, you be shot, in the army, for sleeping on guard duty!"

"Well this here ain't no army, an' you no officer. Better watch yourself Lester." He glared at me, but went on over to his bed roll an lay down. I didn't intend to loose no cattle because of some lazy shirker, even if we had roomed an' whored together through the winter. Both Jess, an' the big fellow George, was grumpy in the mornin'. We had a short breakfast an' moved on. 'Bout noon, after winding through the hills an' valleys, we came to the town of Brookville. It sat upon a hill between the east an' west forks of the Whitewater river. I had the boys hold the herd at the fork of the river an' went on up into town to the sheriff's office, for directions.

The sheriff's name was Mr. Hanna. I introduced myself, as I stepped into the one-room log jail. He arose from behind a small desk an' offered his hand, "What can I do for you young fellow?" he ask, real pleasant-like. He was a big man, with a bushy beard of brown, and chewed a fierce wad of tobacco. He was a excellent marksman at hitting the spittoon by the desk. Had a revolver in a holster hanging across the top of a chair. I told him 'bout the herd to be delivered, an' he right off, gave me directions to the Jackson farm bout five miles east of town. "Take the Hamitlon road here, and go up the hill. It's bout another four miles of beautiful flat country. Mr. Jackson is a tough old bird, but fair. You deliver them before dark and he'll probably put you up for the night in his barn."

Sheriff Hanna then kinda turned to the side an' looked at me outta the corner of his eye, an' said, " Have I seen you before boy? You look kinda familiar."

Surprised me and I quickly replied "No suh, just passed through here awhile back on an army train, but never toured your fine town."

"Why then, ain't you with the army?" he ask suspiciously.

I had to go through the whole story 'bout the sickness an' the accident with the officer. Showed him my discharge papers an' all. He seemed satisfied. We said goodbye, shook hands, an' I left. Felt as if I'd passed muster okay. I figured, he thought that all us dammed 'darkies' look alike, an' he was just doin' his job like any normal ignorant white folk would do.

I joined up with the boys an' we headed the herd east, around the town. Figured they wouldn't appreciate a herd of stinkin' cattle, an' black folk, disruptin' they peace an quiet. I also didn't care to cross sheriff Hanna any more that day.

The two fellows with me wuz ragged-out an tired. They missed the nightly pleasures of the city an was ready to get back. We arrived at the Jackson place 'bout mid afternoon. Wuz a prosperous looking farm with fine outbuildings an' a two story house that was made of brick. Had a front porch with rockers an' a swing. A real comfortable an' first class home.

Mr. Jackson met us at the front gate an' bid us a hardy

welcome. He was a hardy looking man looked to be in his late fiftes or early sixties. "Hello fellows!" he cried, "Looks like old Tommy sent me some first rate heifers! You boys must be fine cowboys! Cattle seem to be in good shape."

I was pleased with his demeanor. " Thank you suh. We'll be happy to putt 'em in the barn, or the pasture for you." I replied.

"Best to put new stock in for a day or two." he answered. " We'll putt'em in the barn and I'll let them into to corral to water later. If I don't hole them up, they might beat you back to Cincinnati!" he laughed. We joined in.

We drove them to the barn.Mr. Jackson put out grain and hay, an' they went right at it. "Well suh," I said after watching the heifers relax an enjoy their meal,"We'll be off an' outta your way if'n that's all you need of us."

Jess, and George were already walking to their hosses.

"Stay the night gentlemen!"Mr. Jackson robustly shouted, " The misses is cooking a fine chicken supper, later you came bunk in the north shed. It's dry, and has an old forge, if you wish to have a fire. You can wash up at the pump, rest abit, and head back to Cincinnati at first light."

I was very pleased, "Why thank you suh. We'd be obliged." Saved us a campout under the cold spring sky. We could make it to Cincy by late afternoon tomorrow. The other two just shrugged, gathered their gear, and headed for the shed.

We made up our beds on old corn shucks and straw on the dirt floor. It was a very comfortable setup. After washing up and relaxing under the chestnut tree out front, we were brought supper by Mr. Jackson hisself. Was a fine meal! We washed it down with buttermilk, and coffee for dessert. We said many thanks to Mr. Jackson. Later the Misses came onto the porch, an' we went up an kindly thanked her many times.

That evening back in the shed, Jess an' George both began

to grumble 'bout missing the city an their women friends. I got tired of listening and said, "Well, ain't nobody stopping you! Jess, saddle up an ride off, if youse so dammed fired up to get back! Should be their by mornin' iffin you ride all night. That is, unless some ol slave catchers get you." There were often groups come up from the south in past years, an try to catch runaways, but that pretty much had stopped, with the war an all.

Jess, started to reply when we heard a sound at the well. A young girl, 'bout fourteen or fifteen years old, was a pumping water for the house. She was the hired gal from the town. Had no family, an' was abit slow in the head, Mr. Jackson had told me earlier, but a good worker. Jess, an' George were getting their first look at her. They glanced at each other, but said nothing. A bad feeling came over me. Suddenly, I wished we'd headed on back that afternoon.

We all three sat in silence on the front stoop of the shed, smoked, an' watched a beautiful sunset. Not much was said, but I could feel tension in the air. Both fellows turned in early. After a short while I did the same. I tossed an' turned abit with unknown worry, but was soon fast asleep.

I dreamed of wooded hills an'stream-filled valleys. In my dream, I walked the woods, an' kept seeing a fleeting glance of the face of the dark skinned girl I'd seen last fall at the train depot in town. She evaded me, but kept popping out from behind a tree in the distance, beckoning for me to follow. Then I heard a muffled sound, again, again…it wasn't in my dream. I woke with a start! Across the moonlit floor, I saw two empty bedrolls. I quickly came awake, got to my feet, an' tiptoed out into the cool spring darkness.

I heard a muffled sound again. It seemed to be from the area of the privy, aways back behind the greathouse. I had a bad feeling in my gut 'bout what the sound was. Sounded like someone in trouble. It wasn't Jess or George making that noise, but I had a bad feeling they was the cause of it.

As I quietly, but quickly, hurried across the close-cropped lawn, a big dog came bounding out the back door of the porch an' headed right for the privy area. Mr. Jackson followed in his night clothes. He had a shotgun in his hands. They didn't see me, so I slowed down an' crept up to the scene. Around the side o the outhouse I could see three people. I heard loud angry voices, an' then the dog yelped, an' came runnin' past me back to the house.

I peeked around the privy, an' saw big George with a pitchfork, an' Jess with a long skinny knife, facing Mr. Jackson, who'd dropped his gun in the scuffle.

The hired girl was layin' on the ground behind my 'former' companions. Her dress was all pulled up, an' her legs was bloody. She was shaking with fear, but not crying out.

"You boys are in it now!" said Mr. Jackson, "Best you leave things as they are and ride on out before it gets worse!"

"No!" yelled Jess, "You the one gonna go! One dead white bastard ain't gonna get us hung no higher!"

George lunged at Mr. Jackson with the fork. I heard the old fellow cry out. He twisted away, as a single tine pierced his side. He grabbed the handle, an' he an' George struggled over it. It was then, that Jess made his move. As he stepped to Mr. Jackson, I came 'round the corner an' kicked as his wrist. The knife went flyin' into the weeds. He whirled at me with a surprised look, an' ran to find the knife. I lowered my head an barreled into Big George with everything I had. He staggered, an' let go the handle. Mr. Jackson quickly grabbed up the gun, an' fired a shot into the air. Everybody froze.

A voice from the house cried out, "What's going on out there?"

"It's alright, Martha!" Mr. Jackson hollered out, "Just an ornery old fox, tryin' to get at the hens! Go on back to bed. I've got some repair work and will be in later!"

Mr. Jackson kept the gun on the two, an' quietly said, "On your knees 'foxes' or I'll gut-shot you both!" They dropped, an' held they hands up high.

"Why suh, we's jus havin' some fun. Ain't no call fo all dis seriousness." said Jes.

"Quiet!" commanded Jackson, "You've violated this feeble young lady. You'll stay put! Lester, would you check on Lilia?"

I went to the girl, who seemed to be in a daze, an helped her to her feet. She shook herself, straightened her dress, an' nodded at Mr. Jackson.

"Alright, Lilia," he said, "Could you go to the barn and bring some ropes. The short ones, by the stalls?"

She nodded, an' quickly left. We all stood as we were, an' waited. Directly, she returned with ropes. "Lester, tie these scoundrels up." I did. Jess complained that it was too tight. George said nothing, but grunted when I pulled the cords tight. Mr. Jackson spoke again. "Lilia can you take Mr. Lester here to the barn, find a lantern, and hitch the mule to the wagon?" She nodded again, an' we headed off to the barn.

The girl was a whiz with the harness an' the mule. We quickly had him hitched up and drove out the barn an' round to the privy. Mr. Jackson had the fellows on their bellies, with his shotgun at their backs. "Let's get them into the wagon." he said.

"What you gonna do wif us?" cried Lester.

"Well boys, I figured we'd ride into town and let you tell the sheriff and townsfolk your story, and see what they decide." he said.

I was in a panic "No suh, please, no sheriff!" I cried, " Only make things worse for all us, especially de likes o' me! We can

CHARLES J. GRIMES

handle this ourselves suh. Ain't nobody gonna miss these two no-'counts."

He looked at me an unnerstood perfectly. "You got spunk boy. Do you have the nerve?"

I nodded. He turned to Lilia, "Girl, go to the barn and get two long hay ropes." She turned, without a word, and left.

"What you gonna do wid us now?" cried Jess.

Mr. Jackson knelt beside the two men and quietly said, "We're gonna hang you son." It got very quiet, except for Big George. He started cryin' an prayin. "Do it quietly young fellow, or I'll give you the butt of this shotgun."

We helped George up an into the wagon just as Lilia returned with ropes. When we tried to pick up Jess, he kicked out at us, an' fought. "Okay young fellow," said Mr. Jackson, "If you don't want to ride in the wagon, then you can follow along." He grabbed a rope from Lilia an' quickly tied a loop round old Jess's legs. He tied the other end to the wagon. "Hop in!" He said to me an' the girl. "Lester, you drive the mule. I'll keep an eye on these boys. Just head out across that field. There's a road on the other side that'll take us to a grove of white oaks, 'bout half mile."

I sat in the seat with the girl beside me. She was quiet an' still, said nothing. I figured she's in a shock, an' jus let her be to herself. Was easy to see with the moonlight an' all. I drove the wagon slowly so's not to bang up Jess too bad. Every once in awhile I'd hear a grunt or curse, but he was lucky, the field been recently plowed an the dirt was soft. Once we got to the road he bounced along over a few rocks, but was mostly dirt and weeds. George was tryin' to sing some ol' spiritual song but messed up the words regular-like.

We finally entered the white oak grove. It was sure spooky lookin' in the full moonlitght. Mr. Jackson told me to pull up

34

under a large oak in the center. They was a huge limb sticking out bout ten feet off de ground. I stopped the wagon under it.

We dragged a very woozy Jess to his feet an hoisted him up into the wagon. He could barely stand. Mr. Jackson fashioned nooses an' tossed the ropes over de limb. He put a noose over Georges' head. I did the same to Jess. He managed to bite me on the wrist as I did it. I yelped an' jumped down off de wagon.

Mr. Jackson tied off de ropes an told them, " You boys can help yourselves if you jump when we move the wagon. A broke neck is a quicker death than strangling. Do either of you have anything to say?"

Big George was half out o' his mind an crying. He shook his head. Jess jus looked at me a said, "See you in Hell nigger!"

Mr. Jackson climbed over the wagon seat an' sat by Lilia. He gave the reins a shake an' de ol' mule took a couple steps forward. Neither man jumped. It was a terrible sight! Those two twisted an' turned. Both drew they knees up, Jess' almost to his chin. They eyes was a poppin' an' tongues stretched out. They kicked sumpin' fierce. Took several minutes, seemed like hours, to be still. Lilia got down from de wagon, walked 'round back an' stared up at de dead. Mr. Jackson came 'round an' pulled her shawl tighter round her, an' put his arm on her shoulder. "It's over now girl. Ain't nobody ever going to know what happened here tonight. She nodded an' looked at me. I nodded an' we got back into the wagon an' returned home.

I didn't sleep much that night. Just sat on de step o' de shed an' thought 'bout dem boys. Seemed like a nightmare had happened.

Guess I finally drifted off, but woke at dawn, found a shovel in the shed, an' walked back to the hanging place. They was still hangin'. Both were a sorry sight. I walked off a bit an' started digging them graves. Even scoundrels deserve to be buried.

I's 'bout half through the first grave when Mr.Jackson showed up. He simply nodded an' started on the other grave. I helped him finish it up. We let the boys down, dragged them over, an' rolled them in. Was a sorryfuneral, but they made they own beds, so let them lay.

Mr. Jackson said a couple religious things over the fresh graves an' then turned to me. "You best come on back with me now, Lester. Mrs. Jackson will have us some breakfast. You'll eat with me in the kitchen. We'll discuss your future." We headed back, tired an sweaty, our deed done."........

I was sitting on the grave When Lester jumped up and bowed. " An' that's how I came to be a Franklin County boy!" he laughed. "Mr.Jackson offered me a job right on de spot. I did have to travel back to Cincinnati, to return the hosses an' pistol to de straw boss, at the pens. Mr. Jackson said it was the right thing to do. Mr. Jackson even lent me a nice bay mare for the ride so's I could get back to the county easier.

We concocted a story dat the two boys had got drunk an' headed out for Indianapolis on a freight train, an' left me to finish up. The boss was real obliged, especially since they didn't get they final pay. He gave me two dollars extra, on top o' my wages! I returned to Indiana in fine fashion."

# Chapter 3

The two of us sat on the old grave and looked out over the valley. I viewed the hills, and saw trails of smoke from cabins, nestled in the valleys. I looked over at Lester, he was smiling faintly. "What?" I asked.

"Oh, I's jus thinkin' bout how fate works in our lives. Bad things happen, then good come out of it, jus goes on and on."

"Cause and effect, right?" I answered.

He shook his shoulders, and said, " I reckon. Every time I's in a fix it seemed to work out, or at least head to a path I's meant to travel on."

"What does that mean?" I asked.

"I'll jus go on with the story, you'll see. It was as if I was guided to this valley for a reason. That reason, is why I'm in dis here fix today."

He sat quietly a few moments, then continued. "Things worked out pretty well for me at the Jackson farm. I's put up in the old shed. We made it into a comfortable bunkhouse. I worked hard, but was well fed an' fairly paid. Mr. Jackson was a good boss-man. Mrs. Jackson, an' her two daughters, were fine cooks. The hired girl, Lilia, she was always quiet an' shy. Never heard her say much, but she would look kindly at me an' smile once in awhile. Never again, was mention made of that 'ugly' night.

Well, Like I said, the work was fine. Sometimes Mr.Jackson would send me to town for supplies an' such. I got to know the area an' meet some right nice people. The grain mill, east of town, was a gathering place for farm folk. While wagons were waitin' to load, or be unloaded, folks would exchange news an' gossip. I got a few strange glances at first, but after a few trips, folks got to know me. Sometimes Mr. Jackson would ride along, just to visit with folks an enjoy life. He helped ease folks concerns 'bout me. There was rumors 'bout strange happenin's at the farm, but I never claimed to know nuthin'. Mr. Jackson took care of all the rumors.

Sometimes, Mrs. Jackson an the girls would go with me. The daughters wuz in they early teens an' loved to spend time in de stores. Mrs. Jackson was a quiet woman, a little younger than the Mr., but a right handsome lady, an' seemed to be of strong stock. Their only two sons had died years earlier, at young ages, of the 'milk-sickness.'

It was a nice an leisurely time, awaitin' while de ladies shopped an' browsed. The girls flirted with town boys, but Mrs.Jackson kept a tight rein on them. Poor Lilia never left the farm, to my knowledge. Dat girl had a whole lot o' loneliness in her soul.

Sometimes, Mr. Jackson gave me the afternoon off, jus to myself! I liked to take a bag o' bread an cheese, ' an walk the hills 'round de valley. I enjoyed the views from the balds. Those's places where years before, farmers had logged an' burned off the timber an' brush. They drove the cattle up to those high places for the good grazing. They'd be an occasional granddaddy-oak, or maple tree, to set under an' enjoy the afternoon. Sometimes I'd leave the highlands an' walk the valleys, along the cool damp streams. The noise of the gurgling waters would put me fast asleep after many a lunch break.

There were glades of trees along the streams, where a man could wile away his days, enjoyin' the wildlife, deer an' turkey with an occasional fox on de prowl, or jus' doze in a sunbeam, dat fell twixt the trees. Once I even found rock-hard giant bones of a big-type animal. Mr. Jackson said they's from ancient times, when giant animals were around here. I figured those ancient people must've had plenty of eatin', or got eatin' plenty!" He laughed at his joke. He sat a bit, quietly sighed, then slowly and seriously, started again.

"Well, one late summer afternoon when the chores were all caught up, an' evenin' work aways off, I decided to head out for a walk. De Misses gave me a rucksack of food. I thanked her, an headed out for the area north of the town. De Misses, she was always good to me. I think she was grateful I's there to help out on that terrible night, but none of us ever mentioned it.

As I said, I headed for the valleys north. They was two of them, divided by huge hills. the valleys worked up to the flatlands 'bout a mile north. As I walked up the valley, directly up from the center of town, I followed a small creek that tumbled over riffles an waterfalls, as it worked its way south. The noise of the stream, an' the buzz off bees an' the crickets, filled the air. "Bout half mile up a ways I smelled woodsmoke. "Mus' be somebody's campfire." I thought, an' walked toward it.

I walked a ways, an' came to a small clearing in de woods. Came to a place dat looked like de remains of an old homestead. All dat was left was de old fireplace an' chimney. I could see they was a fire going in the fireplace, an' bending over tending it was a woman. She wore a long dark skirt, had a snow white blouse, with a bright red vest over it. As she stood, her long black hair fell below her hips. It was raven-black, an' tied in a ponytail. She was a dark skinned lady. Her shiny golden earrings sparkled in the sunlight. She was well built, an' had a small waist. A beautiful woman!

I was looking through de brush, an' had jus decided to call out, so's not to scare her, when she turned an looked directly into my eyes an' smiled! I nearly fainted! She was de girl I'd seen at the depot last fall!

She stretched her arm an' motioned to me to come on over. My legs were like lead an' I couldn't move. "Come to me, dark man." she smiled an' said. I slowly shuffled into the clearing an' stopped, a few feet from her.

She stood there, smiling an looked me up an down. Then, she stared into my eyes again. Her eyes were like black coals, they seemed to pierce into my soul. She spoke, "I 'been expecting you. Sit, and join me for a bite to eat." I was dumbstruck! "Lester, Lester," She laughed, " You're with a friend. Sit and relax." She motioned to a large rock by the fireplace. I sat. She tended the fire an' stirred a pot, that sat in the nearby coals.

I finally got up de courage to speak. "How'd you know my name, girl? An' What you mean, you with a friend, an' you been expecting me?"

She laughed. Was a deep chuckle way down in her chest, made me uneasy. "I knowed youse in the area, 'afore youse in the area. I knowed of your adventures an' strolls. See'd you often in the woods. I knowed you'd come, sooner or later."

I was nervous an' leery of dis girl. Never heard no mention of her in de town. I did recall seeing her last fall, but never since then.

She turned back to me with a wooden bowl in one hand, an' a spoon in the other. "Here, have some stew with me, boy, then we can do business. You're not afraid of me, are you?"

"No, no," I stuttered, "Jus' abit surprised to find such a pretty girl like you way up here in de woods. How you know so much 'bout me? An' what you mean, by business?"

She laughed again, showing her pretty white teeth an' de dimples in her cheeks. "Enough talk for now son, eat." She reached behind her an' returned, with a tin cup, "Here, have some of this fine dandelion wine."

"Sorry mam'," I said, "I got chores to do later. It wouldn't be good to show up at de farm with 'hard drink' on my breath."

"Oh," she said, "Just a little sip won't hurt. Helps the food settle." I took the cup.

The stew was tasty, abit spicy for my likes, but good. I sipped the wine. It was like honey. The best I ever tasted! As I finished the stew an' wine, she pulled out a jug an' refilled de cup. I tried to resist, but she insisted. I slowly drank an' watched her eat. Guess I got drowsy an' lay back in de grass a spell. Must've dozed abit, cause when I woke up it, was getting dark. I felt abit woozy. She was building up the fire. "Oh sister!" I said, as I propped my elbows under me. "It's late I gotta run to get back for chores!" She jumped up an stood over me.

"No, we dance now!" she said.

"Dance?" I cried, "Girl, you crazy? I gotta get back 'fore Mr. Jackson skins me alive, an' sends me on down de road!"

It was then I heard the strange music, comin' from somewhere. Was wild an wonderful! She playfully pushed me back down an' began to whirl an spin. De music began to pick up, an' so did her dancin'. She started slowly, then picked up her pace with de beat of de drums. It was an ungodly mixture of music of drums, fiddles an flutes. As she spun an' jumped 'round the area before the fire, she motioned me to join her. I shook my head an' stayed down low. I's too amazed by the carryin' on, and bewildered by the music.

It was then, she began to strip of her clothes.The vest went aflyin' with her hair ribbon. Her long black hair was scattered over her shoulders. Next she ripped of the blouse top, an' whipped it away with a fling. What a sight!Her dark breasts bounced with the rhythm of de music. I was spellbound! Next, she whirled 'round an stepped out o' de dress. Nuthin' under it but flesh!

I couldn't move! She danced, an' spun round naked in the moonlight, like nuthin' I'd ever seen before. I was excited, if you know what I mean, an' couldn't hide the fact. She made an big turn an' then jumped right astride me. I pulled her to me! We rolled in de grass. She took me again an' again, til we exhausted ourselves, an' lay together before the fire. I slept.

My dreams were filled with wild music an' fire! I saw the demons from hell adancin' before me. The devil hisself, danced up an' thrust his old forked tail at my face. I tossed an' turned, before I finally woke, in a cold sweat.

It was a foggy mornin'. She lay asleep beside me, the embers of de fire still aglow' in the early light. My head was a poundin'. Was it from de wine, de woman, or both? I was in trouble! Had missed last night's chores, an' sinned, with liquor an flesh!

I rolled away from her an' got to my feet. She woke, an' jumped up in a tizzy. She leaned close an whispered, "What you gonna do now, boy? You mine, now. I got your soul, your manhood!" She laughed.

As I scrambled for my clothes, I kept an eye on her. She's like, she was crazy! "I gotta get,woman! I done messed up bad. Shoulda' never been here with you! What's so funny?"

"Why, you mine now, boy. You never get away. Was it good?"

I was tryin' to get dressed. Barely got into my britches, was pullin' on my braces, "You de best girl, best I ever had, but I gotta go, an' fast."

She stopped smilin' an' said, "You the best I had son, an' now you gived me the best, to have again!"

I was confused, "Say what? You talkin' crazy girl!"

She stood naked before me, an' stared, seemed to look right through me. "You family all de same. You like your father, an' his father before him. You all got de sign!"

"What sign?" I asked. Now, I's really scared. She reached out her hand ' placed it behind my neck, an' pulled my head to her. She slowly ran her hand up to the back o' my head an' stopped.

"There it is!" she shouted. "You got de knot of de 'Melungeon'! You got the mixed blood of de ages, son! The blood of all mankind. You be lucky, you be unlucky, but you never be bored!" She took away her hand an' walked back to the coals. As she bent over an stirred them, I turned away, so as not to see her womanhood again. Was too much to handle for me. I finished dressin' an gathered my things.

As I made to leave, she turned an stood, hands on hips. She dropped a shoulder an' pointed a long finger at me. "Yes, you like all de others. I knowed your great granddaddy, your granddaddy, and your daddy, an' now I knowed you! I recieved life from dem! I gave life to dem! I took life from dem! I be your grandmother, great-grandmother, an' mother. Now, I be the mother of your child!" She turned an' bent down, an' pulled up an old dress. As she turned back, what I saw made my hair stand up straight! She was an old wrinkled woman, of great years. Her hair was grey an' whispy. Her flesh hung in wrinkles, from her neck an face. She stared and gave a toothless laugh, as I cried out to God!

"Won't do you no good, boy!" she cackled, "Your god not be listinen' to you today. You done gave your soul to the Devil!" She pulled open the dress, to reveal the same young body I saw before. She slowly closed it, an' she appeared to be very old and wrinkled. "You boys with the mark, 'be special for my work. I 'be sent here on a regular basis to 'recruit' for de boss, de Angel from hell. Too late for you, boy." She laughed, "Your soul be lingerin' in eternal damnation, but your seed goes on in this world, to feed needs in the future!"

"Oh Lord," I cried, "Now, I saw her again in my memory! Her dark eyes an long black hair, as she nursed me as a child. I saw her rockin' me as a baby. I saw her leavin' me with those neighbor folks. She was ageless. A witch from Hell, that cursed me an' my ancestors!

"You can't leave now, son." she said, "Be needin' you round to help out in the future. I promise you eternity fo' life, for your help." She smiled an' motioned me closer.

I saw all de pain an' agony of my life before me. She was the reason for all the lonely years of wonderin' 'bout family. I saw the reason for my hurt. As she let go with another laugh, I lunged at her, an' grabbed her neck in my hands. She was strong, for an old bitch, an' we wrassled 'round abit. She got her arm between my wrists, an' broke loose. I kicked at her, an' as she dodged, she tripped an' went down hard. She hit her head on the hearthstone by the fire, and was silent. I slowly knelt beside her still body. Her head was broke open, she was kilt! Red blood mingled in her long, grey hair. I had blood on my hands an' wiped'em on my britches. That's when I heard de dogs!

# Chapter 4

We sat in silence on the old grave. He hung his head, in sadness and shame. I tried to console him, "Lester, it seems you got into a crazy mixed up mess, that wasn't your fault. She took advantage of you."

He shook his head, tears streamed down his cheeks, "No, it be my own fault. Shoulda never let things go that far. Her beauty an' the wine got me all messed up. I let it happen. It was, as if it was meant to be. It was what put me here!" He pointed to his grave.

"They hung you, didn't they?" I said.

He nodded slowly, and began again, "Was hunters in the woods. Three of 'em, an' a passel o' dogs. They came up the valley an' found me by the woman. Both o' us covered with her blood. They didn't ask no questions, jus' hoisted up they guns, an' marched me off towards de town. 'Fore we got outta de woods, we ran into an bunch o' rowdies from de mill. Dey was on dey way to work. When dey heard de hunters story, dey didn't wait fo' no sheriff or law. Jus' throwed a rope over a tree limb, an hauled me up! Was a terrible thing. I strangled, slowly. I kicked an tried to scream, but nuthin' came out. Felt as if my head was gonna bust, an' then all went dark." He sat and cried softly, "I never meant no harm! It all happened so fast, jus, over."

"So, that's your story." I said.

"No, not all of it." He looked coldy at me. "Next thing I remember, was a voice callin' me, 'Lester, Lester, come on up, Lester-boy. Come up an' open your eyes. I know you.'Well, I opened my eyes, an' was a sittin' on this here grave, jus like you an me are now. I saw dat ol' man over there (He pointed to Isaac's grave). He was asmilin' at me an' sittin' in his rocker. He waved me on over. I could hardly walk, but shuffled over to him. He was real nice an' gave me a hug. Said he knowed of my troubles an' he listened to my story. We sat a long spell an' talked. Felt good to share with a 'kindred' soul. He explained alot of things to me, then he told me his story." Lester hung his head, tears dropped upon the damp grass.

"What's his story?" I ask, "What's he have to do with you?" He didn't respond, just sat crying and shaking his head. "Lester.......?" I ask.

He raised his head, and had a faraway look. He gazed across the valley and said, "Have to ask him. It's his story, an' some of mine." I shook my head in amazement. He explained...... "He be my father."

"What?!" I exclaimed. "How can that be? He died in the 1820's! He was eighty-three years old!"

Lester shook his head at my stupidity, "Look white boy, I's somewhere in my thirties when they hanged me. He was alive when I's bred. 'Sides, that old devil- woman can do strange things to a man of any age."

"Unreal!" I thought, "These guys didn't need Viagra! They

needed saltpetre! Must've been in the water!"

Lester grinned across the grave, as if he read my thoughts. "You have to listen to the ol' man. He tell you his tale. I be gone now. See you later." He vanished before my eyes.

I arose, and hurried across the graveyard. As I walked quickly by Isaac's grave, I felt his presence, but kept walking on out the gate, and into modern-day life. I needed to clear my mind and get a grip on reality.

I walked on towards my home to the north, glad to be free of the past, but with a heavy burden in my chest. What a story! What a nightmare!

At home, I did my writings in my journal, I did mention of the strange events of past weeks. I prepared for classes and tried to focus on the events at hand, but was distracted, and often 'off in my thoughts.' My wife simply dealt with it as usual, only asking if things were okay, and how was school.

The next week was a blur of classes, students papers, and chores at home. I was in a fog. Occasionally, I would gaze from my second story classroom over the old cemetery, wondering if there really was something there or if I was simply losing my mind. I would be excited at times about hearing the rest of the story, but also scared about what lay in store for me.

Finally, on Friday after school, I decided to have another go at it. My week had been fairly normal, no 'ghosts or goblins' haunted me in my waking or sleeping hours. Maybe it was just a figment of my imagination, or, maybe they were over there, quietly awaiting my return. I had to find out. After the students had gone, I descended the two flights of stairs, went across the street, and entered the past again.

"Took you long enough to work up the nerve, young fellow!" The old man said, as he rocked away in the chair. "We thought you were never coming back, after the scare you got from Lester's story." He laughed.

"What's a week, when you've been here for over 170 years!" I was miffed at his impertinence. After all, I was the one supposed to help them. He leaned forward in the rocker and gave me a look that made the hair on my neck stand on end! "Don't mock me boy! Times a wasting, and we have none to waste. We need to get on with this, or it'll pass us by again. Lester and I, and many others, have been through this several times. It's a real blow to miss an opportunity. Means years of untold misery for us all!"

"What opportunity?" I asked.

"What opportunity?!" He incredulously raised his eyebrows, and arched his back, "Why, the opportunity to be released from this darkness. This limbo of nothingness and despair! This may be the opportunity to set things right, if you have the stuff about you!"

"How, am I the answer to your problem? What can I do?" I cried.

He leaned back in the chair and let out a deep breath, "Son you won't have to worry about finding the problem. It's already found you. You just have to be able to deal with it. What did you think of Lester's sorry tale?"

I shook my head in disbelief. "It was unbelievable, I mean, the parts where you are his father, the young/old witch woman, and he said, he killed her!"

"Hah! He thought he killed her." Isaac gave a grim chuckle. "They went back to retrieve the body, but it was gone! A bloody trail led off into the woods. They figured a bear or wolf carried her off, but we know. She lived on, to carry out her dastardly deeds, in future years. Hard to kill off a devil-child."

"In future years?" I ask, "You mean she lives on yet, today?!"

"Relax for now, son." He settled back into the rocker. "Best you hear my story an' then we'll discuss the situation." He lowered his head, as if in deep thought, and then quietly began to speak.

"They believe I was borned 'round 1737, in Georgia. My family roots are a mystery to me. I's told, there was a wagon train of three families headin' through the foothills, when they were attacked and massacred by Indians. The neighbor folk saw smoke, and heard gunshots. They tried to rescue the poor folks, but by the time help arrived, the redskins were ascalpin' and taking goods. The neighbors ran them off with a few musket shots. They searched the area and found all dead, except one, a newborn baby, saved only by its' mother and father's bodies, which covered it. That baby was me.

I had survived, but there was no identifying items around or in the wagons. The poor folks had been heading for a new life and a new start. I guess none were much on writing or saving legal documents. I was an unknown, doomed to live under someone else's name, and share someone else's history.

Luckily, a fine Piedmont family, the Saynes, took me in. They had seven children, but accepted me as one of their own. When I was old enough to understand, my adopted mother told me of my past, but said only, that it was best left behind. I was one of them now, and would always be so.

I grew up on that little hill-farm. Did chores and worked hard in the fields alongside my father brothers and sisters. It was a good life. Sometimes, preachers would travel through and stay for the night. The next day they would bless us with a fire and brimstone sermon, and be gone. Funny thing was, often, they would shun me. Take a look at me, and turn away. They'd whisper things to my parents when I was out of earshot. Sometimes there'd be an angry exchange between my father and the preacher. The fellow would pack up, and hurriedly go on his way. When I ask what was wrong, my parents would kneel before me and assure me things were allright. Some people, they said, were hippocrits, who didn't accept others just as they were. They told me that I was fine just as I was. I never really understood until later. Was too much for a ten year old to understand, anyway.

One day, we were in the field pulling stumps, when we saw mamma Sayne come across the way with dinner. It was the usual, bread, cheese, water and a pie. The old mule stopped pulling on the stump that we'd hitched her to. "Just leave her be for now, boys." Poppa Sayne said, "We'll eat a bite an let her rest up. She'll pull it out, directly."

I walked behind the mule to unhook the tow chain when, Whap! She kicked out with a rear leg and caught me alongside the head. Next thing I remembered I was in the dirt, dazed and bleeding. Poppa and the boys quickly unhitched the mule, led her off, and carried me to the house. There was blood over my face and shirt, my head felt as if it had caved in. Still have a scar under my right cheek!" He pointed to it. A thin white line ran from his ear, along the jawbone.

"I was laid on a makeshift pallet before the fire. The sisters got damp rags from the wash bucket and cleaned the wound. Momma said I'd be fine, and for them to just go on back to the field, and she'd tend to me. Everyone said nice things to me. Older brother Jed even chided me 'bout getting out of work. Poppa twisted his ear for that, but it was in fun.

Momma kept a damp cloth over the cut and cradled my head. "You'll be marked son but won't hurt nuthin, just give you character' she said.

I ran my hand along my sore neck and head. As I touched the back of my head, I felt a knot protruding from the base of my skull. "Momma, that mule cracked my head an' left a lump! There's a bone stickin' out!" I cried.

She lifted her hand to the spot and sadly shook her head. "No son, that's your 'special knot.' You had it as a baby when you came to us." I looked at her in wonder. She said, "It's called, a Melungeon Knot."

"A what?" I asked fearfully.

"The Melungeon knot is the mark on a special people. You have the blood of peoples from all over the world. Maybe a mixture of kings and princes. Spanish, Portuguese, French, Indian, and…maybe African." She pulled me abit closer and said. "Son you are different from most of us. Notice how your skin darkens so quickly in the summer sun. You have a beautiful brown color. Your raven black hair and dark eyes make you a pretty sight. You are our handsome one!"

"Is that why people sometimes whisper 'bout me momma, when they think I don't hear?"

"Son," she said, as a tear formed in her eye, "People can be cruel and prejudiced at times, even men of the cloth. They don't understand that we are all God's children, no matter what background we come from."

"But momma," I cried, "I just wanna be like you and poppa and the others! I don't want to be different!"

"Hush child! Poppa and I call you 'our special one' because of your knot. You must never reveal it to the others, and never share this secret with anyone. People don't understand. They fear what they don't know about. Melungeons are special people with the blood of many races. They have exceptional luck, both good and bad. You are strong and handsome. You have the intelligence to make something of yourself. Someday, you'll leave us to strike out on your own. God left you for us to raise up, and to set free into the world, to be somebody. Poppa and I brung seven beautiful children into this world, but gave us you, as a project, to prepare for greater things. We knew it, and now you know it. Others would be jealous of your gifts if they knew. Yes, soon you'll have to leave us to find your true destiny. We have you for only awhile.".... Tears rolled down her cheeks as she hugged me.

"How'd you know all this 'bout me, momma?" I asked.

"Child, stories abound in these hills 'bout your type folk, strange, magical, mystical stories. You'll live an interesting life if the facts hold up. Folks can see it in your features, in your eyes, in your character. You be blessed with this burden." She said no more, just rocked me in her arms, and hummed an old tune to herself. I gazed into the fire and occasionally reached back and touched the knot. It was the first time I pondered the strange abnormality, but not the last.

# Chapter 5

Isaac sat back in his rocker, and pulled an old clay pipe from his pocket. He didn't light it, but rolled it around in his hands, and touched it occasionally along his scar. After a brief rest, he began again. "The years went by quickly on the little farm in Georgia. They were the best of my life. Had family, and plenty of good work during the day, with good food and a warm home at night.

When I was in my late teens, I got the itch to go. We all knew it was time. Two of my older sisters had married and gone off, long before they were my age. My oldest brother was 23, but stayed to work the farm with poppa, and leased some land nearby. I had decided to head east, to Savannah.

I had made the fifty mile trip to the seacoast city several times. Took the wagon for supplies two or three times a year. Sometimes we'd sell any surplus crops we were lucky enough to harvest. I always enjoyed the strange sounds and noises of the city. The clop clop, of horses hooves on cobblestone streets, and the chatter of the street vendors and buyers, sounded like the 'buzz of the busy hive' to my ears.

I was most of all taken by the great sailing ships that came into the harbor from all over the country and across the ocean. Strange and different men sailed these vessels, with even stranger cargo. The smell of coffee and cane from the Indies, the chests of tobacco loaded from the docks, and black slaves from Africa. I was bothered a bit by the sight of human beings in chains and treated as livestock, but was no real business of mine.

It was an early summer evening, after the planting was finished, that I told momma and poppa of my plans. I hoped to find work on a ship and travel the world. They was both sad at my leaving, but realized it was time. The little farm could support only so many, after all, and I would be one less mouth to feed. Still, there were a few tears and extra special hugs, before bed.

On a bright and sunny morning, a few days later, we said our final good-byes. Five of my seven siblings were on hand, with momma and poppa at the doorstep. Many hugs kisses were exchanged. Although we were not of the same blood, we were closer than many who are.

Poppa shook my hand, gave me an embarrassed sort of hug, and tried to sniff back a tear. Momma waited until last. With eyes glistening, she hugged and kissed me. She put a hand on my neck, ran it slowly up to the base of my skull, and stroked the knot. She whispered, with a pained and hoarse voice into my ear. "You are special, always remember it. You have a mysterious blessing upon you, and are destined to travel and have adventures. Use the gift wisely." She broke the embrace, and went quickly into the house.

Sad, and a bit confused about mommas' talk of blessings and gifts, I tossed my sack of belongings over my shoulder, picked up my walking stick, and with a final goodbye, headed out. After several yards, I turned and looked back. They were all standing together, silently watching me. That is my final memory of them. I never looked back again. I covered the fifty miles in less than three days. I was excited, and pushed hard. Slept in the woods by the road both nights, without any adventures. It was coming late in the afternoon of the third day, that I came within sight of the town. I decided to pitch camp by a small stream, wash up and present myself in proper fashion the next morning. It was a cool night, but I was hot with excitement of my first venture into the real world."

He hung his head, and sat awhile in silence, "Many's the day, when I wished I'd turned back that next morning and gone home, to that small hill-farm."

He sat in quiet meditation for abit, and then continued. "I was in high spirits when I entered Charleston, that next morning. I slowly walked the streets and took in the sights, sounds, and smells of the city. The shouting of drovers, street vendors, and buyers sounded like a 'gaggle of geese' to my unrefined ears, but was pleasant and comforting. The smells of the bake shops made my stomach growl, but I'd had a breakfast of biscuits and salted pork, and hoped to hang on to the little money I had. No tellin' what was in store.

The smells and sounds from the blacksmith's, and stables, rang true to my nose and ears. They were familiar to me. I could smell the salty sea breeze as I neared the wharves. The tall masts of the ships at dock were an overwhelming sight. Although I knew nothing about ships or the ocean, I was determined to try my luck, there, in the strange and fascinating world of faraway travel. That's where my destiny lay, I thought.

I stopped at each gangplank, inquired about work, and was rudely set on my way. I was getting dejected, when at the fourth ship at the dock, I finally had some luck. There was a grizzled old cuss sitting on a small barrel. His long thin hair was pulled tightly into a ponytail. He wore three-quarter length trousers, and a dirty long sleeved homespun shirt. The fellow had a quill and paper, and was pouring over figures. He was tryin' to count barrels and add figures, but seemed to be in a tizzy, mumbling and cursing to himself.

"Can I be of help, sir?" I ask.

"Be off with ye lad!" He cried, "I've enough troubles without yer interrupt'n'. Captain'l have me hide if the 'Bill of Lading' doesn't talley!" He made a 'shooing motion' with his free hand.

Well, momma and the older sisters had seen to it that all us boys knew readin', writin', and 'rithmatic. I figured this was a chance to show it off. "Beg your pardon sir." I interrupted, "I'd be happy to 'sifer' for you, as you count the tally. I can write fairly legible, and it'd make the job a sight easier on you."

He eyed me suspiciously, "Now, why would a fine young gentleman like you, want to help the likes o' me, with my work? You be a beggin' food or somethin'?"

"Oh, no sir!" I replied, "I'm lookin' for work of any kind, and would be glad to be given a chance to show my abilities to you, even if things don't pan out."

He hesitated, and the cautiously handed over the papers and quill. "Don't knock over the ink bottle, and write them figures so's I can read them!"

"Yes sir!" I proudly exclaimed. He began to count and call out numbers and contents. In a short while, we had the task accomplished. Hogsheads of tobacco and rum, bales of cotton, and indigo were all tallied. As he took the papers and checked my figures, a smile broke out in he craggy face. "Well done." he said, "You ever been to sea?"

I hung my head, and hesitated to answer. He broke the uneasy silence. "Never mind son. We're a bit short handed, as it is. The crew usually goes ashore for leave, and as luck would have it, one or two usually don't get back. I'll speak to the Captain today. Be here at sunup tomorrow, and we'll check the situation out. If Captain says we need you, we'll be setting sail with the morning breeze."

"Thank you sir for the opporunitly! I shall be prompt!"

He laughed, "Yea, you be prompt, and be ready for work." He extended his hand, "Jean Cobre," he said with a smile.

"Isaac Saynes" I said, as I shook his hand. He nodded, and turned back to his work. I turned, and walked off with a much lighter step, as I headed towards the market for fresh food for the day.

I spent the remainder of the day taking in the sights and sounds of the city. I walked and wandered. A right lively place. By late afternoon, I made my way to the west 'bout half mile and set up camp in the cane breaks, by a creek. It was a wonderful evening. A blanket of stars above, and the night sounds all round. I finally fell asleep by the fire and dreamed of seagoing escapades, adventures, and faraway places.

Early the next morning, I awoke in a foggy mist. It was damp and chilly by the stream. I quickly ate my last biscuit and a piece of jerky, and gathered my things. As the sun rose over the horizon, I was heading into the city.

All along the wharves people were beginning to stir. Many, looked the worse for wear, from whatever happenings they'd been into the night before.

I made my way to the rendezvous at the ship. The name "Golden Leaf" was scrolled on her bow. She lay, as she did the day before, except most of the cargo on the dock was gone.

Coming down the gangplank was a young boy, carryin'

chamberpots to be dumped along the shore. "Pardon me lad." I said, "I'm looking for Jean Cobre. Do you know him?"

"Aye," said the boy, with a grin, "He was bedded down last night on the afterdeck. Might still be there." He pointed the way.

I made my way up the plank, onto the deck, and headed in the general direction the boy had pointed. I walked around some barrels, and saw a figure in blankets on the deck. He seemed to be mumbling something to himself, and stirring a bit. I gave a hardy hello, and the scene quickly blew apart! A naked and startled, Jean Cobre jumped to his feet, as another figure on the deck yelled, and pulled the blanket over her bare breasts! "Whoa Jean! It's only me Isaac Sayne!" I yelled, as I raised my hands in preparation to defend myself.

He shook his head, and a bit of recognition came across his face. With an embarrassed shrug, he said, "Damnation Lad! You scared the 'be-jesus' out of Milly, and me here! We was havin' a mornin' wakeup before she left. Who the hell gave you permission to come aboard?"

I pointed to shore, "The young boy with chamber pots."

Cobre grinned, "Ah, young Sckully, the captain's boy. We must be gettin' ready to put out early today. Milly, off you go, and thanks a-many for the sportin'." He grabbed the blanket off the poor wench, as she scurried about the deck for her clothes. Now that all the 'goods' were in the open, she dressed, unembarrassed, before us. Jean tossed her a coin and bade her farewell, until his next trip. She gave me a wink, and a toothless grin as she walked by. "Not much on looks, but she can sure stir a man's coals!" He laughed. "Come on, we'll meet the captain, and then we'll eat."

"I've done eat." I said.

"Nonsense!" he said, "You're dam near broke, and liven' on

travellin' rations. I can tell but the 'sink' in yer gut. Come along, and I'll buy your first meal as a seafaring man."

"Does that mean I have a job?" I ask.

"Aye, it does. Seems two of the mates got in a scuffle yesterday, over a whore, and cut each other up pretty good. Won't be shipping out with anybody fer awhile."

I was excited, "When do we sail?" I ask.

"Hopefully, not until you and I can rustle up some grub and a bit 'o ale." He slapped me on the back and off we went to the captain's quarters.

The meeting with the captain was brief. He was a huge man, with a black beard that hung to his chest, and long black hair, tied back into a tail. He seemed busy, and was anxious to be off. He shook my hand, after Jean's introduction, "Emile Cartier," he said, "I expect my men to work hard! Are ye up to it?" I nodded. "Then be ready to sail within the hour." He went back to his charts. We headed for the nearest tavern.

After a breakfast of biscuits, gravy and strong ale, we made our way to the ship. My stomach was unsettled from the drink, but I tried to hold up and pay no mind. The crew was already hurrying about, with Captain Cartier shouting orders on the main deck. He gave us a stern look as we ran up the plank. "Not had enough whoring yet, Jean?" He bellowed.

"No sir, I mean yessir, just took a bit of nourishment to tide me over!" yelled a laughing Jean.

"Heave to gentlemen!" The Captain cried out. "We sail for the northeast with the tide!" Everyone seemed to be in assigned places, but me. Jean quickly pointed to a rope, and I pulled with all my weight. We slowly were moved from the docks, pulled by two boats of rowers. The men strained, and headed the ship into the harbor. Immediately, others scrambled up the tall masts and unfurled the sails. The morning breeze filled the white sheets and they billowed. It was a wonderful feeling to be under way!

The gray-white sails snapped-to, and the ship gained speed. The rowers untied the ropes and pulled off. We were a sail! With the fresh sea breeze in my face, I looked back to Savannah with a feeling of destiny achieved at last!

The old man lay back deep into the rocker with a haunted look in his eyes.

"Done for today?" I asked.

"No son," he quietly replied, "Just remembering, one big wrong, after another."

# Chapter 6

The first two, days the weather was fine, as we sailed north along the coastline. I was busy with the scrubbing and cleaning, above and below decks.

The ship appeared clean, but a distinct smell pervaded the air. Cobre', said it was from the slaves. This ship was a slaver that had made several trips across the big ocean, to Africa, and returned with it's hold packed, with black slaves.

Cobre' said they were horrible, nasty journey's, of screams, illness, tears, and death. He had made two such voyages, with one as terrible as the other. He told me of the dancing of the slaves... They brought them above the decks from the cramped quarters below, and dowsed them with saltwater, to clean and heal the sores they bore. The sailors also had 'their way' with the young women, while above deck. Some women tried to jump overboard to certain death, rather than submit. Schools of sharks followed the ship along its' journey, in order to feed on the bodies that were frequently tossed overboard. Many slaves died...The fish ate well.

Cobre' seemed so moved when telling these sad tales, that I ask, why he'd participated. He replied, "Riches my boy! Vast riches and profits, to be made by those of us, who'd otherwise be paupers!"

They sold the slaves in the Indies Islands, and purchased sugar cane and coffee, to be sold in the Carolinas and New England. They would stop off in Savannah to sell coffee, top off the fresh water barrels, have a bit of relaxation, and then head north, as we were now. Luckily, the holds that I now worked in, were packed with coffee and sugar, but there was still that smell of death and sorrow that seemed to creep out of the wooden hull. Along the walls were chains and manacles, stored for future use on those poor people.

The third day out, the skies darkened, and we pushed out away from the treacherous shores into deeper waters. A terrible storm hit us at midday. The sails were quickly hauled in. However one poor fellow slipped from a yardarm and fell to the deck below, severely breaking his leg and arm, as he bounced off the solid wood planks. Screaming with pain, he was quickly carried below. The captain was up near the helmsman barking orders. I quickly went below, and prayed to God to deliver us. It was a long afternoon and evening, as the ship was tossed about the sea. Water streamed through the belowdeck seams. I slept, but little. With the coming of dawn, the seas calmed. The wind and rain died down, but our trials were just beginning.

As the first rays of the morning sun streaked down to the hold, I heard the hurried scramble of feet, and urgent voices. "Bloody pirateers!" Came a wild cry from above. "All hands stand to! Man the guns and trim the mainsail!" I hurried up the steps to the deck, just as a cannon shot burst from a nearby vessel. The ball traveled across the short distance and tore through the railing at the bow of our ship. I was terrified! I ran to Cobre, who was helping shove one of our two small guns to face the menace.

"Where did they come from, Jean?" I cried.

"The bloody devils must've sighted us from shore. The storm blew us back to it. Appears to be 'Nags Head.' A terrible bit of luck for us. 'Tis a veritable 'Pirates den' there. Help us lad." We pushed the bulky cannon into place and a charge was loaded. Sails were unfurled, as we attempted to outrun the fleet pirateer ship, but it was a feeble effort. They came upon us quickly. Our fellows managed to get off a shot, but their cannons made fodder of us.

The mainsail was splintered, with it's mast breaking in two and falling across the deck. The ship pitched and I was hurled across the deck into a stack of empty kegs. As I attempted to dislodge myself, another ball skipped across the deck and into the kegs, blowing the entire mess, myself included, overboard. I must've been unconscious for a bit, 'fore when I came to, I was floating a couple hundred yards from the ship. My arm was looped through a rope that held three kegs together. Guess that's what saved me from meeting "Davey Jones!"

There was more cannon fire, and small arms fire, and then all was quiet. The 'Golden Leaf' was surrendering. The Pirate ship tied-to and men boarded the captured vessel. I heard cheers of victory and screams of agony, as men celebrated, by vanquishing their foes. I saw Captain Carter hauled up to a yardarm by his neck. He kicked and twisted a bit and then was quiet. Just as it appeared he was dying, the rope was released. His body fell forty feet to the deck, and bounced very high. Next, I saw his head, and then corpse tossed overboard. Was a sickening sight! I never knew the fate of my friend Cobre. Possibly, he survived and joined the pirates. I never saw him again.

My left side was bloody and full of splinters from burst kegs. There appeared to be a gash on my forehead and left cheek. The saltwater ate at my wounds. As darkness fell, I secured my hold to the kegs. The last thing I remember thinking was, "If I ever get to safe land, I'll never go to sea again." I blacked out.

# Chapter 7

I awoke, squinting into the sunlight, at the scruffed and bearded face of an old black man. He was leaning over me examining my features, as I lay in the warm sand. The waves pounded the shore, as the surf swept up and around my prostrate body. My head was full of pain. My arm, and wounded side, throbbed mercilessly. I drifted off again.

I next awoke in a dark, but warm cabin. I was on a makeshift cot of seagrass on the floor. A wrinkled grey-haired black woman was attending to my injuries. She cooed softly in a strange 'Cajon-like' accent, like I'd heard before, when bands of European gypsies came through our farm, in years past. It seemed many years had past since I'd been on the farm, although it had been but a short time. The pain in my head was but a dull throb, but my side felt afire, as she deftly pulled splinters from skin.

She looked at me and gave a toothless smile, "Hey mon," she said, and then nodded, "You come back from de 'nither lands', at last. We tought you gonna leave us a time or two." She placed her hand behind my head to lift, so's I could drink from the cup she offered.

"Oh Lord!" She cried, as she dropped my head back onto the pallet, with a thud. Blue light of pain, flashed before my eyes. "He's got de mark, Jerrol!" She cried, as the old man came quickly across the room. "He's got de headknot, Jerrol!" The old man slid his hand behind my throbbing head and quickly removed it.

He stood and looked down at me. "Boy, you be blessed and cursed." He softly said, "You be of de old ones, both good and bad. Have much luck in life, you will boyo, but de luck be both up an down fo you. Wonderful things, terrible things. You be melungeon!"

Although still dazed, I remembered my mother's words, and ask the old man to explain his talk.

"Melungeon!" He said louder. "Boyo, you be born o' de blood. Have great luck, good and bad, all yo life. You be star crossed, star cursed! De be no rest fo you none 'o your days, boyo!" He looked to the old woman, and said. "De voodoo blood be strong on him. Have all de signs. Too much, for here. Must leave!" He turned, and quickly headed out the door.

The woman looked worried and tired. She arose, went to a far corner, and returned with a corn husked doll, and a jar of a paste-like stuff. "Be best if you close de eyes. Let Matilda do de medicine." She dipped her forefinger into the jar and pulled out some of the paste. She rubbed it into the head, and side of the doll. I closed my eyes.

Soon I felt a cool soothing relief throughout my injured body. A great fatigue came over me and I drifted off, to hazy dreams of drums, firelight, and dancing bodies.

I awoke much later. It seemed to be daylight outside. I felt surprisingly good. My Head pain was gone and as I inspected my side and arm, they appeared nearly healed. Beside me, lay the cornhusk doll, wrapped in rags and blood-spotted. I was alone in the cabin.

I lay back, and tried to make sense of what had happened to me. Was all this real? Was this a bad dream? Maybe I was still at home, and delirious. Then, the door to the cabin opened, and the old woman appeared. She wore a shawl over he worn, calico dress. She' been a beauty at one time, but the years and toil had robbed her of her looks. Her long grey hair was still thick and full. Her dark wrinkled skin was weathered, but she looked to be strong beyond her years. Great veins protruded from her forearms.

"Aha!" she cried, "You be better! We get some broth into yo boney body and some strength back to you." She went to the fire and ladled a bowl of chicken broth from a caldron. I was able to sit up and slowly drink. It was heavenly. She looked sadly at me, shaking her head.

"What?" I ask.

"Best you heal quick, and be gone. De bloody pirates find out 'bout you and we all be in fo' it. De bad men all 'round dis place. Dey don bother Jerrol an me. We harmless, but if de find you be hiding here, den de be hell to pay!"

"I need to find my ship." I said. "We were being attacked and I was blown overboard. I think she was boarded by pirates."

She sadly shook her head, "De ship, she be layin' in de sand under de waters. You friends, de be feedin' de fishes."

"My God!" I cried, "All of them? Everything is gone?"

"Aye, happens all de time 'round here." she gently said, "Dis water be death to passers-by. De pirates take bloody bounty, an leave us in peace. De believes we give dem luck an' good fortune. If de find you here, all is over."

"Have you been here all your life?" I ask.

"No, we be from de Indies islands. I was taken as young girl, from homeland far across de ocean. Made de death trip of many weeks. Was taken freely by de filthy sailors, when we's allowed up top. Left de homeland a young girl, come to de Islands, a grown woman. Worked de cane fields and did fo de misses.

She was in a quiet trance for a bit, and then continued. "An old witch-woman showed me how to get through de pain of slavery. Showed me dark magic… voodoo. Can take de pain… can give de pain!" She chuckled. Escaped de islands after a few years. Sneaked onto boat, and ended up here, at dis banks area with my man. Nobody bother us, live quiet, is nice.

She was again quiet, and I started to lay back, when she grabbed my arm. "Hear me boyo. Hear me good! You be special. You be of de blood! Maybe some of us in you! De head knot tell de truth. Now lay back, and drink dis." She placed a chipped bowl of dark liquid to my lips. It was thick and bitter, but strangely soothing. "Lay back and sleep. Dream, and remember." As I drifted off, I looked into those ancient eyes. They danced with firelight.

I dreamed of dark peoples, of kings and princes, of wild whirling dancing peoples. I was one with them. It was a dream of colors, and flying, swirling, rainbows of cloth. We were wild, wicked, and free!

I must've slept through the day, for it was dark outside when I finally awoke. There was a bedroll and a leather sack by my pallet. The old woman and her man were sitting in chairs quietly watching me. As I shook the cobwebs from my mind, the old man leaned close and said, "Time for you to go boyo. You be sore, but able to travel. I paddle you to de mainland, an' den, you strike inland. Go den, to de north, do not stop fo' long while. Best we be off soon."

The old woman gravely nodded. She got up and helped me to shakily stand, an' get my legs under me. She gathered the bedroll and foodbag, and helped me to get ready. The man went outside.

As I stumbled through a sorry 'thank you,' her eyes filled with tears. She reached out a boney hand to my cheek. A warm glow came across my face as she slid the hand around behind my head, and caressed the knot. Her eyes rolled back, she tilted her head far back, and said, "Oh spirits be wit dis po' soul, and guide him on his journey through life. Fo' he be a special one, an' need your help. We always be wid him. He never be far from us again." She withdrew her hand and turned away. Without another word, I left the cabin.

# Chapter 8

After the old man deposited me on the Carolina shore, he quickly left, with hardly a word. Glad to be rid of the trouble, I guess. I headed north, but stayed along the coastline. There seemed to be roadways of sorts, and I made better time. I passed only a few people and made little conversion. I was eager to leave this area of hellish memory. My seafaring days numbered less than a week, but left me with a lifetime of nightmares.

After a few days the meager supplies began to run low. I worked up the nerve to stop by lonely cabins and work or beg for food. The people were poor, but generous. I always had food and often shelter in a barn or lean-to. I told people that I was seeking my fortune in the north. All seemed eager to hear news of the road. I told them what I'd seen (Minus the sea escapade), and exchanged stories for their goodwill. After many days, and cold damp nights, I finally arrived in New York City.

The city was not the 'wonder' it was to become, but it was a 'wonder' to a poor country boy. There were many Dutch and Swedes, intermingled with the English settlers. There were strange accents and customs. It was all very hectic. I did not spend a night in the city, instead, I quickly passed by the docks as unpleasant memories came back. I headed on, to the north. To make a long story shorter, I ended up in the colony of Massachusetts.

I had a wonderful tour of the east coast and its' people. Most were friendly, but the best, was there in the 'old colony.' Boston, was a busy seaport city that I enjoyed for a couple days, but I pushed on to the north. I figured not to stop, 'till I got to the top of the world and take my chances there. I was halted in my journey by the beauty of the New England countryside. It was a beautiful summer's walk, with the breeze blowing through my hair.

My hair, was the source of amazement to me. It was shoulder length and thick. I stopped by a pond to wash up, when I noticed my reflection in the pool. The long, once dark strands, were beginning to turn grey! The person I saw, was no longer the fresh back country boy from the canelands, but an older, more experienced man. My life threatening experiences had changed me, both without and within!

When I arrived at the village of Lexington, a few hours walk from Boston, I was pleased with the area. A town of a few clapboard houses, with a commons, for grazing animals and loafing. I felt that I had arrived at my destiny. I found work on the farms around the area, and ended up the summer by indenturing myself to a miller, named John Coopersmith.

I did plenty of good work for the man, and met many people of the area. They were mostly hard-working farmers who cared not for who you were, or where you were from, but for the labor you performed. My hard work and dedication was noticed. T'was the year 1766.

I worked three years for miller Coopersmith. After my

indenture, I was able to work out a rental agreement with a wealthy farmer who had many acres, and was happy for it to be put to use.

By the summer of 1774, I had purchased 60 acres of my own, and built a cabin. I had a "going concern," and was well thought of by the locals. I was also courting a local girl, Miss Abigail Harris, from Lexington town. Her father owned a tavern, and I often stopped by on my way in for supplies, not only for an ale and supper, but just to glimpse 'fair' Abigail. She served the meals with a smile. I worked my way to a wink, and that led to a visit with her and her family a time or two. Folks of the area were friendly, but a bit slow to 'buy in-to' someone "lock stock and barrel." I had to proceed in my 'amorous ways' with caution.

Things were also perking up throughout the colonies, at this time. Seems the mother country was putting more and more demands on colonists, such as taxes and rules, that we had no say in passing. The taxes on various goods and papers didn't affect me too much, but I heard plenty of grumbling at the tavern.

There'd been killing in Boston back in '70. Called it a massacre. British soldiers had fired into a rowdy crowd and killed five. There was a big uproar and a trial, but not much that affected us.

In the autumn of '74, a group of representatives from the various colonies met in Philadelphia. Seems there'd been a lot of trouble after a bunch of locals dumped British tea in to Boston Harbor. There were fights between colonists and soldiers, and among the colonists themselves. A local rebel-rouser named Sam Adams, attended the congress in Philadelphia, and came home with stories of possible rebellion or reconciliation with the Crown. Though he preferred rebellion.

It was soon thereafter, that local communities began to call out and organize militias. They all marched around and played at military tactics. Seemed ridiculous to me! I didn't care much for the Britishers messing with our lives, but they were our sovereigns, and had the most powerful army and navy in the world. I decided to steer clear of the "play army", and just wanted to be left alone. That's, when I learned what a "shunning" is. The locals were very cool towards me. Some called me a Tory, or Loyalist, for not taking their side, but most just ignored me. Well the 'Hell' with them, I thought! I'd seen first hand, what superior firepower can do to the less powerful. The hidden scars on my side reminded me of the agony of battle.

Things changed with Abigal, also. She was 'terrible' saddened by the things said 'bout me.I finally gave in, and talked to some of the boys about joining up. I was to be at the next meeting of the militia, when all hell broke loose. T'was late in the night of 18, April 1775.

# Chapter 9

It was a quiet spring evening. I'd worked the fields hard, all day. Had a sore back, and even sorer foot, from where the old plow horse had stepped on it as I was removing his harness. The big toe bled a lot, an' it raised the toenail. After limping around an' russltin' up supper, I took a 'hit' off the corn liquor, soaked my poor foot, banked the fire, and turned in early.

T'was sometime late in the night, when I heard a horse a galloping up the road at a hard pace. The rider was ahollarin! I hobbled to the door, but couldn't make out his words, as the fellow roared by in the dark. Was headin' west towards Farly's farm. I figured it was his youngest boy Jacob, who sometimes got too much into the liquor, and let off steam late at night. Went back to bed, and fell into an uneasy slumber. My foot felt afire!

Some time later, I heard horses from the west and voices. Went to the door and gave a hollar. "Hail to ye, fellars!" I cried, as I limped into the front yard. The riders pulled up. T'was Farly and his boys Thomas, Nathaniel and Jacob. Also, the Smith brothers, Josiah and Edward, were along.

"Hail to you Isaac!" said Farly. "Old 'Sam' get your foot again?"

"That he did!" I called, "Probably loose the nail and a night's sleep over it. What's happening' with you boys at this late hour?"

"Didn't you hear the rider?" He called, "Britishers are marching full force up Lexington Pike. They appear to be headed for Concord, and the munitions we've stored there. Isaac, we need every man to take a stand on the Commons. We're heading in to sign the muster book."

I understood the challenge. Was time to put up, or be forever shunned. Visions of a crying, and ashamed, Abigail, were in my stupid head. "Give me five minutes!" I said, as I limped to the house for my gun and powder. Soon, we was headed for Lexington.

We arrived before dawn, to see a large group of men and boys outside the meeting house. They had queued up, and we joined the line. We all signed on, to the 'Lexington Alarm Company.' There was bout 150 of us, all totaled. When my time came to sign the ledger, I gave my full name "Isaac Saynes," all got quiet and eyebrows raised. The commander, Colonel Lattimer, hesitated, then stood, and put out his hand. "Welcome neighbor, glad to have your help." I shook his hand and felt proud to be among friends again.

As the April morning sun came up over the horizon, the whole 'ragtag' bunch of us gathered on the commons. Colonel Lattimer formed us into two rows, one behind the other. We stood at ease and listened, as he explained that we were to hold fire when the redcoats arrived. We did not want trouble, but only to slow them, and to give our friends at Concord a chance to hide the guns and shot we had stored there. We stood in our crooked lines and waited. Some men smoked clay pipes, some chewed a bit of leaf. A few nervous words and cautious laughter took place, and then the local dogs that had gathered for the show, stood at point and began to bark. Then, we heard the drums. The noise they made sounded like distant thunder, and kept getting closer.

Oh what a sight it was, when the perfectly straight red lines of soldiers came round the bend in the road! They all had bright red coats, with cross bands of white. The foot soldiers wore huge bearskin hats that made them look ten feet tall! There was a bit of fidgeting among some of the younger fellows. Colonel Lattimer tried to keep calm by repeating, "Steady boys, steady boys, steady boys…"

The lobster backs halted before us. The drums were silent. I remember the sounds of the birds, in the nearby trees. The chirping was quite a contrast to the scene before us. An officer rode up, and began to scream and shout for us to disperse, and lay down our arms. Colonel Lattimer tried to talk with him, but he was adamant, and quickly wheeled his horse and returned to his troops. Next thing we knew, they was forming up into ranks across from us, fixing bayonets, and the drums changed cadence. They began to march towards us with a tremendous shout, "Huzzah!"

More then one man embarrassed himself by breaking wind, and a couple 'lost their water.' I stood firm in the second rank, and cocked my gun. The fellows began to lose nerve and walk backwards. Young Tobias Edgerson, tripped and dropped his cocked rifle. It went off. All hell broke loose! There were many more shots, from both sides, as men began to run in disarray.

As we turned and ran, the bullets flew by! They sounded like bees. There were screams from men, and from within the shuttered houses, nearby. I found myself running beside Josiah

Farly. I turned, just in time to see his face ripped apart by a ball. Blood and brains flew over me! He crumpled, I ran on like the wind! Forgot all about my sore foot. Made it past the out buildings and into the brush beyond. Ran bout a quarter mile into the deeper scrub and lay hidden. I listened to the moans and screams of the wounded. Men begged for mercy, but were bayoneted, and left in agony. The British soon turned back, not wanting to fight in the woods. They reformed slowly. Officers were screaming orders and slapping at soldiers with swords. There was an occasional shot and then all was quiet. The drums began their marching beat, and the troops moved on towards Concord. It was over in minutes.

"My God," I thought, "'Twas a slaughter! No quarter given. We were at war!" Then, I heard the sharp wails of the womenfolk, for their loved ones. Was a sad sight as they staggered across the green grass, to the dead and wounded. I arose and vomited. In my shame, I turned and ran deeper into the woods. I wandered to a creek and began to throw water on my face. It was then, I realized I'd been wounded. Was just a graze. A nearly spent bullet, had penetrated the skin of my left ribs. The place where the splinters had been removed years before by the old voodoo woman. I took my knife and slit the skin, the bullet fell out onto the ground. I removed my shirt, and lay in the shallow water. It soothed the wound. After a short time, I got up and packed mud over the wound, and moved on.

I must've been travelling for an hour over the hills, when I came to a rise overlooking the Concord road. I saw, and heard the British coming along, and then saw movement in the brush, behind the rock walls along the road. There were many men in hiding. As the British came alongside, the fellows opened fire. Several redcoats fell and the men scattered into the woods. Several came arunning past me, yelling for me to get moving.

Before I turned to run, I saw a small group of lobsterbacks running up the hill. I took aim and fired at the lead soldier. He was thrown back into the men behind him. As I spun 'round and ran, it occurred to me, that I'd just killed a human being!

# Chapter 10

The skirmishes went on all throughout the day. We ran along the hills and pastures, and took shots at the bright red targets. I'd fire and run, reload on the run, find another see-through spot, and fire and run again. My blood was up! It was no longer a human endeavor, but a bloody conviction, to wipe out the enemy! We were finally 'winded', and gathered in the hills, and waited for the British to return from Concord. They'd apparently had a rough time of it there, and were hurryin' back down the road to Boston. Their retreat was made even more agonizing by our well-laid ambushes. We were elated! Every man believed himself to be, 'God's Avenger'! I'd fire and retreat to the cover of the brush, and make my way southeast. I'd stop to shoot, when I got to a wall, or cover along the road.

Late in the afternoon, as I was running through a wooded copse, I tripped, and fell nearly into a stream. As I started to rise, I noticed a movement in the brush across the water. I slowly crept forward. It was a wounded redcoat! He was younger than I, leaking blood from three wounds in his chest and belly. His death was near. As he struggled to move away, I tried to calm him, and lay down my gun. He stared at me through pain-glazed eyes and said, "We don't belong here. I want to go home." I knelt, and lifted his head, and gave him a sip of my water. He mumbled something about his mother and a girl, but soon passed into sleep. A bit later, as the afternoon died, he did too. He gave a last long breath and went limp in my arms. I sat by him in the growing darkness and was ashamed for us all. What kind of people were we? This man had traveled thousands of miles, only to meet his death by a lonely creek, in the backcountry of Massachusetts. For what did it gain him? I closed his vacant eyes, as mine filled with tears. I took rocks from the creek and covered him so that varmints would have hard time getting to his carcass. I lay his hat on the makeshift grave, and went on. Life would never be the same.

I wandered in a daze, up and over hills, until I came to an area I recognized as being near Lexington. As I crested the rise, I saw a glow in the darkness. Thinking the British had torched the town, I ran on, down and across the fields. When I came within sight of the area, I realized that the glow was from a huge bonfire on the Commons. Folks were gathering there to grieve together, and greet those who were returning. My horse-crushed foot was ailing something fierce! I limped into the gathering. Several turned towards me and gave me a hearty welcome. Old Tobias yelled, "The hero of Lexington!" and everyone gave a cheer. "What are you talking about?" I asked.

"We've heard of your exploits, Brother Saynes!" Reverend Farr exclaimed. "You gave those foreign devils 'hell-for,' all the way up Concord road and back. Several of the returning men have told of your heroic deeds, and of saving our boys from the enemy. You are a true community hero."

I was appalled! I ran with the others from the Common

earlier in the day with the first gunfire, and hid in the woods, until my teeth stopped chattering from fear. As I ran away further, I was drawn into the 'melee' with the others. It was simply survival! I was no more a hero than anyonelse! I received the handshakes and backslaps, with silence. As I looked around, I saw houses with candles in windows, and quiet movements within. No heroic deeds could return those husbands and fathers to their families. I turned away from the gathering and walked towards home. Mr. Smith yelled, "Some of us will be heading out for Boston in the mornin' to give the British what for! Sure could use a fighter like you Isaac!"

I nodded and waved, and limped on back up the road to the cabin.

It was late in the night when I finally arrived at the homestead. I checked my animals, built up a fire, put a poultice on my aching foot, and one on the ribs. Couldn't sleep, so I sat up, and relived the day's events. Finally, I must've drifted off, because I dreamed of dead soldiers, and of running through the woods in terror. The old Carolina woman appeared in my dream and spoke to me. "You be special boy. Special good an special bad!" She laughed. I saw the dying British boy, crying and shaking his head in fear......

I awoke with a start! It was dawn, the ashes were cold, and I was very stiff and sore. My decision was made. I would only be trouble for my friends in this fight. They would suffer more for my being there, than my absence. I would head out for the western territories.

# Chapter 11

As the day began to wake up, with sleepy sunlight peering through the morning mists, I loaded my two horses, one for riding and the other with gear. I took my deed for the property, tucked it into my vest pocket, and headed to the northwest, for Concord. A feller there had inquired about the farm a couple of times. I figured if he was still in the market, that I'd make him the deal of a lifetime!

As I rode in the damp misty fog, I felt guilt and sadness, at leaving behind the life that I'd come accustomed to. My friends and acquaintances would be mystified, but it was for them, that I was leaving. I always managed to survive the rough times, but those around me suffered. I was a jinx, a misfit. They would go on just fine, without me.

My mind also wandered back to my adopted family, down south in the Savannah canebrakes. I hoped they were all fine. Somehow I felt that my leaving them was just in time, and they would have grown and prospered by now. I felt free, and ready once again, for a new beginning.

In Concord, I quickly found Edgar Jones. He was a hard working blacksmith, who dreamed of escaping to the farm life. Although hard times and uncertainty were coming, he readily jumped at my proposal and we struck a deal. I sold the place lock, stock, and barrel for a small sum of cash and a British musket he'd confiscated, along with ample supply of shot and powder. I now had money, two guns, two horses, and supplies,... and my freedom. After spending the night at his family home, I headed out the next morning, for new territory.

I traveled by day, and camped along fresh streams by night. It was a beautiful spring, cool and dry. Made my way across the colony and headed southwest, along the ridges of the Alleghenies, across New York and Pennsylvania. There were beautiful areas, and nice people, but I needed to be free and alone. The folks I encountered at the settlements and homesteads were considerate and hospitable, but seemed to be relieved, as I bade farewells.

I soon discovered the cause, when I stopped by a quiet pond to water the horses. As I knelt to 'wet my whistle', I noticed my reflection in the mirror-like water. I hardly recognized me! My long hair was nearly white, although I was a young man. My face had a hardened look, the eyes deep, dark and sad. Yes, I looked as if I was a lost and wandering soul. Looking back on those days, I often wonder why, I never bothered to take time to ask God for guidance or help. Guess I figured I was on my own from day one, and would go on that way... How wrong I was!

Well into the summer, I crossed into the Appalachians and Virginia territory. After weeks of travel and living off the bounty of the land, I'd slowly moved into the high country and came to the western boundary where the Ohio river cuts along. I was on a high ridgetop and could see the river snaking along in the distance. In the hills beyond was Indian territory...

trouble! I decided to pull up, and stake out a claim right then and there. It was beautiful country, with plenty of game, and most of all… solitude.

I immediately started building a cabin, and planted the seeds I'd purchased in Concord in a small clearing nearby. Though it was late in the season, I hoped for the best, and worked daily in my little garden plot. I'd work on the cabin abit, and then hunt for game. I salted and dried meat, cleaned and dried hides. Wood was cut and piled for the winter, as the cabin slowly took shape.

The cabin was a small, 14 x 12 foot affair, with a stone fireplace along the south end wall. I split cedar shakes, on and off, throughout the summer, and by fall had a 'snug' cabin, with a fine shingled cedar roof. I managed to harvest a small amount of beans and corn from the poor ground and stored them, along with a few pumpkins and squash, in the root cellar I'd dug behind the cabin. It's amazing the work a man can get done when he has to! I was ready for the winter, a real mountain man!

The winter of '75/'76 was rough up on that ridge. Never before, did I feel the chill of the wind as bad. I'd haul in firewood and keep the fire blazing. At night, I slept before the fireplace, bundled in furs. On the coldest nights, I'd bring in the horses. Was a powerful smell in the cabin come mornins', but cozy! Never did think I'd see the springtime, nor never longed for it so much.

The creeks froze up and I'd melt snow for water. Had plenty of food, but had to scrounge forage for the horses. They came to enjoy eating certain types of thawed out tree bark. All our rations were limited as the winter wore on.

By the spring thaw, we were all abit gaunt and rank. Don't know if I smelled like them or they like me, but we survived. If'n a stranger would've stopped by for shelter, he'd probably chose the blizzards to us, but we were comfortable and reasonably warm.

Christmas was a lonely time, but I did read to the horses from the 'good book', and tried some feeble prayers. Come warm weather, I did truly thank God for our deliverance!

Spring finally came. The creeks freed up and the waters rushed noisily along the rock-strewn gullies. Birds came to life with song. It was a glorious event! The cycle of clearing and planting started over.

I lived on that mountain top for over twenty years. Though I seldom saw a living soul, it was a haven for me. An occasional Indian or two came by, and I'd 'parlay,' feed'em, and trade goods. I heard of Indian troubles after the war, but was of no concern to me. I got along just fine.

I made a couple trips each season to a nearby settlement called Wheeling. I picked up the year's supplies, bartered furs for goods, and got the recent news. Seemed the 'Britishers' got the worst of it from the boys, and George Washington was a hero. He been made President, of our new nation. I now lived in a State, Virginia. I wondered what would have happened if I'd gone to Boston, back in '76, but realized it was for the best. I'd brought trouble to somebody for sure.

Being up on that ridge top was lonely at times. I did miss occasional human companionship, especially of the 'female kind.' Solitude does have its virtues. I tried to talk to my Lord, but never seemed to get anywhere. Felt guilt and sorrow about leaving the folks in Massachusetts, but made the best of the life I had.

Near the turn of the century, I was nearing my fiftieth year on this earth, and feeling the need to do more. Things were right peaceful and comfortable on the homestead, but more and more I'd see people travelling to the west. There were settlers movin' close to my place, and a road that cut through a nearby pass, Dunnmore's Pass, they called it. Looked like Dunnmore's Hog waller most of the spring and fall. Was mud up to axles in places. People seldom stopped, especially once the Indians were pretty well whipped. I figured that before I took up the rocking chair for good, I'd best have one more adventure......It was the mistake of my lifetime.

# Chapter 12

Was the spring of 1800, a new century, and time for a new beginning for me. I was 49 years old, and eager to get along. I'd spent the winter pondering on the affair. Come warm weather, I made a trip to a nearby trade post and cashed in most of my stores for cash and supplies. I now had a good horse and a pack mule. One sunny April morning, I just loaded up and rode off to the west.

I was amazed at the number of folks I met along the way. When I first traveled to this place, years ago, I was a lone frontiersman. Now I was just another traveler. Made my way to Wheeling, and crossed the Ohio on a ferryboat. Making my way at a leisurely pace, I passed through many settlements that were becoming regular towns. Finally came to Losantaville, or 'Cincinnati,' as it was already being called. It was a growing concern, at a bend in the Ohio, and many stopped to resupply and move on. Many stopped to stay.

At a small trade post I met with a grizzled veteran of the wilderness. 'Said he'd lately been up to the Indiana territory.

'Said it was a bounty of good cheap land and plenty of wildlife. Injuns, had been recently pushed further to the west, and troubles were few. Seems the Greenville Treaty had pretty well opened up the southeast area of the territory for settlement. I was ready. It sounded like a place of not too many folks, and a climate more suitable for my weary bones.

It was a paradise! I traveled three days up creeks and valleys into the rolling hills of southeast Indiana. On the fourth day, I came to a peaceful valley where the east and west fork of the Whitewater joined, to form one river. It reminded me of my former mountain home, a miniature version.

There were a couple campsites upon the rise between the river forks, and others being set up. I stopped and talked to the folks. They seemed right friendly. A fellow named Butler, was platting out the land for a town, and told me of land to the north of the camps. I rode on. Came up to the crest of the hill to the north and encountered flatlands. 'Was amazed at the change in the lay of the territory. Seems years ago, tons of ice from the north had pushed south, flattened the area, and began to recede, just at this point! A "Holy" ground indeed. I felt I was home.

I traveled back down the valley and filed a claim with this Butler fellow. He seemed to be the 'head man' of the area. Set me up a campsite up to the north of the valley, between two hills. 'Was sheltered from the wind and had a small creek that flowed down from the north.

That summer I built my cabin. 'Had learned a lot from my previous homestead experience, and did it right. By fall, I had a cozy cabin, with a big creekstone fireplace at the north wall, and a lean-to for the livestock. That spring, I'd put in a garden in the fertile lowland soil nearby, and had a decent harvest. Was a glorious summer of work and exploration of the area.

Over the next couple years, I met a few people as they came

and went. They were surveying the land and planning for their future. In 1803 had my first neighbors. A fellow named John Conner had set up a trade post earlier, about six miles to the south. He was an 'industrious' fellow, and had a Delaware Indian wife, and her kinfolk living with him. He built a mill further north along the river.

I enjoyed my visits with him and his kinfolk. He'd been raised up in the 'old frontier' and intended to do big things in the trade business. A few years later, he packed up and moved the entire concern 'bout twenty miles to the northwest, to a place along the Whitewater that eventually was named after him, Connersville. 'Never heard whether he made his riches or not.

They was also a couple Frenchmen named Telier and Peltier, who set up a trade post just above the east fork of the river, on a little rise. They was a bit more difficult to deal with and I stayed away from them.

I also found out that I had neighbors to the northeast. They was Scotch-Irish peoples, who were friendly, but kept to themselves. They had cut a trail called the 'Carolina Trace,' clear up from the Ohio river.

In 1804, this Butler fellow returned, and settled land a mile south of me, where he'd had his earlier campsite. Things really began to pick up, with new folks coming in 'regular-like' and putting up cabins. By 1808, a town was forming. Butler named it 'Brooksville' after his mother's maiden name, later the "s" got dropped and here we are!

I was pretty much content to be a good neighbor and help out the newcomers, whenever ask. Although I was a loner and considered abit 'curious' by most, they also considered me to be an authority about the area since I'd been over most of it.

As I grew older and more content with life, I came to enjoy

sitting at the 'gossip bench' in the town square, by the log jail house. On lazy summer afternoons, the old fellows would all gather, and we'd swap stories about our travels and tell 'whoppers.' I made up some good ones!

Spent some time at the Yellow tavern. Spent one night in Sheriff Hanna's new jail, after too many drinks, and a disagreement with a young fellow over the War of Independence. I was 'plowing a furrow' through a passel of the boys, when the Sheriff showed up and quietly escorted me, and the instigator, to the cells. We both woke up the next mornin' with black eyes and wounded pride. Shook hands in front of Sheriff Hanna, and he let us go with a chuckle. Life was easy and restful, with a bit of fun tossed in.

I never really struck up a relationship with the ladies of the town, since most were married. I did visit a lonely widow woman a few times, just to let off a bit of 'steam.' Close female companionship was not what I needed at this age, just my peace and quiet.

'Father time' was a-catching up with me. I lived here for over thirty years and had nearly forgotten the 'Melungeon curse.' Thought that maybe I'd outlived it. I had finally been through all my trials…. How wrong I was!"

The old man sat for a bit and rocked quietly in his chair. There was a cold dark stare in his eyes. I sat without speaking, content to let him think.

# Chapter 13

He leaned forward in his rocker, his energy restored…. He spoke.

"I was in my 83'd year. It was a wonderful autumn, of sunny, warm days, and cool nights. I knew my 'time' was near, but did not care, for I'd thoroughly enjoyed my thiry-four years in this little valley. Had seen a lot of changes, and an actual town grow up around the area. It covered some of the hill between the river forks, and spread down east into the valley by the East Fork.

We'd become a county, in 1811, and an actual State, in 1816. Was a grand occasion, with revelry for days and nights! Folks ask if I'd 'stand' as a representative to the State Convention in Corydon, but I said I was too old, and had no desire to travel that far. Things had been too good. I didn't want to 'tempt the fates' and mess up good, again. I did think of the past, now and then.

Then, the past began to come back! I had dreams, of pirates and redcoats, and running in fear. I'd awake in the middle of the night, drenched with cold sweat. The bad times had been away too long, and were coming back to me again.

It happened on that cool autumn evening in '32. I was sitting on the front porch of the cabin, overlooking the town. I could smell the sweet wood smoke from their home-fires. I saw a few lights, from the homes on the main street as they glittered, dreamlike, through the trees. Then I heard a soft voice, from across the clearing. Was a woman's voice, with a southern accent, and a touch of 'Cajun twang.'

"Isaac." She called, "Isaac Saynes, you come on over here to me, boy!" I jumped from my rocker, limped across the porch, and squinted into the darkness.

"Who's out there?" I hollered, "Come on into the light, so's we can talk proper!" My neck hairs stood on end, as I saw movement in the brush. A figure appeared, moving slowly, like the mist through the trees. A beautiful young dark-skinned girl walked into the clearing.

She smiled a beautiful smile, spread her arms, and slowly turned completely around, in the dim light of the clearing. She had waist-length, cold black hair, that shone like coal. She wore a white cotton blouse, with a blue vest, and a red calico skirt, down to her ankles. She slowly glided over to the porch and looked up at me.

She smiled again, and the words poured out like thick molasses. "Ah, boy, you lookin' fine tonight! Been doin' alright fo' yourself all dees lonely years."

I shook my head to clear the cobwebs of age. "You know me, girl?"

"Know you?" She cried, " I healed you up an put you back together after what dem no count pirates did to you! I set you on de path to freedom! Now you remember me?"

Shaking my head and waving my hands, I said, "No, no girl, that was many years ago, and an old woman of the Carolinas. I don't know who you are, or what you're up to, but I'm not in the mood for riddles!"

She laughed, threw up her arms, and with a spin and a cloud of smoke, she was suddenly the old Cajun woman, of the past! She stood before me with her withered arms clasped across her chest. I stumbled back, and fell into the rocker. I closed my eyes and was sure I was having a 'spell'! That often happened to folks of my years. My heart pounded wildly in my breast! I arose, stumbled into the cabin, and slammed the door shut, tight. Walked to the fireplace, and stood there trembling. I heard a soft chuckle behind me, she was there, old and wrinkled, with white hair.

"You think you came jus' walk away from Sheba again, young man! Des no way! When I see'd you the first time, I knowed youse my destiny, but had to send you along. 'Was not de time. Sheba wanted you all dees years, an' have come back for you!"

What in tarnation is the story with you, woman? I hardly knew you then, and sure as 'hell' don't know you now! What do you want with me?"

"Sure as 'Hell', is de right words boy." She laughed, with a gleam in her eye, "You be special. Don' you 'member me tellin' you dat? Got dat melungeon mark on you. You be special boy, for special task."

"What task?" I cried, "And why, do you keep callin me, boy? I'm into my 80's!"

"I show you!" She spun round again. In a flash, she was the beautiful young girl. She reached out her hand, and said for me to take it.

As I stood before this apparition, I slowly shook my head. "I'm old and tired girl. Go and find you a younger suitor."

"Take my hand!" she commanded.

I reached out slowly and touched her soft flesh. It was warm and wonderful. Suddenly, a powerful surge of energy passed through my withered body. My hair seemed to stand on end! My muscles cramped, bones and joints popped! I let go her hand and staggered backwards.

She smiled at me as I looked at my hands and arms. The swollen arthritic joints of my fingers, were gone! The blue veins on my arms had disappeared. There was dark hairs, where white had been. As I shook my head to clear the vision, I realized I was seeing much clearer now. The colors of her dress jumped at me! I glanced at my shoulder-length hair, which was now black, and thick again. My hands reached up to touch the skin of my unlined face. I was truly young again! What's happened!" I cried.

"Now, you be ready fo' Sheba." She softly said. "You feel de force of a young boy. Feel de 'zip an' buzz' in you now?"

I truly did, and was eager to prove it!

"Dance wid me boy!" she began to twirl and spin to a strange music that somehow filled the small cabin. 'Was a haunting rhythm of song, that caught me up in the spell. She ripped of the vest, unbuttoned the blouse, and off it came! Her bare breasts, glistened with sweat and bounced, as she whirled about the room. She stopped before me, let go the drawstring of her skirt, and jumped out of it. She was bare naked as she approached. "Come to me boy, an' Sheba show you de delights of de world. De world, you wuz made for!"

I practically leaped into her arms! We spun about the cabin and fell in a laughing heap before the fire. We made passionate love. It was the night of nights, for me. All the long years of loneliness, washed away in the arms of this beautiful seductress!... Finally, we slept.

# Chapter 14

"I awoke with a start!" He said. "The dim grey light of morn', was just beginning to filter into the cabin. Beside me, lay the beautiful young girl, still in slumber. My grey hair, once again, lay across my shoulder. I staggered to my feet, and went over to stir the ashes of the spent fire. My ancient joints ached with fire. My back was bent, with the agony of misuse. I felt all of my 83 years.

I heard her stir, and turned slowly to see her stand, and begin to slowly dress herself. As I watched her cloth the beautiful body, I once again shook my head in wonder. Had this all been a dream or nightmare? What happened to the youth and vigor that had filled me the night before. "What happened?" I asked her.

"What happened, what happened?" she cried indignantly. "Old man you took me! Took me hard, several times!" She was angry, and her coal black eyes filled with fire.

"No, No!" I cried. "It wasn't that way! I meant no harm! Please…"

She nodded, and quietly asked "Do you care for me?" I dumbly nodded, "Do you love me?" I nodded again, knowing this was a ridiculous mix of young and old.

"Ha, ha!" She threw back her head with laughter. " I have you, old man. You gave me your heart, your soul, your seed. You be de father, of de child of de Devil!"

"What are you saying?" I cried. I could hardly understand her crazy talk.

"I tol' you old man, years ago, dat you be 'wickedly' lucky. You be special!" She circled round me as I stood frozen in my tracks. "I be sent from Satan hisself, to be bred to you. I create sons fo' de devil, de world over! Your manhood be part o' de devil now. Your seed, be his. De devil says thanks!" She laughed, and spun round the cabin.

I didn't know what was going on, but knew this 'bitch' was crazy, an' affix 'en to make trouble for me. Then I heard the dogs,… barking up along the ridge. Was the Eversole boys, on their morning hunt. I knew things were gonna turn bad.

She rolled her eyes up, and to the west, as if she could see through the cabin walls. "Now old man, you luck done run out! You had your good time, and now time to pay de piper! I tell dem hunters how you took Sheba against her will!" Drops of blood appeared across her dress. She tore her blouse and laughed. "I tell dem how you ruined my maidenhood. You gonna hang old man!" She whirled and turned to the door.

I grabbed for her and she spun from my feeble grip, but tripped, and fell headlong against the hearth. Her skull popped, with a cracking sound. She lay silent, as dark blood poured across the hearth and sizzled in the coals.

I heard the dogs coming closer and the voices of the hunters calling. My mind was in a frenzy. There was a thunderous roar in my chest and a catch in my throat. I fell to the floor. The last thing in life I remember was the cabin door opening, and someone coming in.

# Chapter 15

I sat in the grass, as the old fellow silently rocked. His eyes closed against the torment. All was quiet. He did not seem inclined to offer more so I ask? "You died?" He nodded. "What about the girl?"

He barked out an exclamation, "Heh! They never found no girl. Was just my cold body. Seems to them, I'd been dead several hours. Heart attack and old age. They buried me with military honors.. 'Cause of the old 'war tales' I became a local legend. Faded into history, and forgotten.

I lay here in my grave, trapped in this limbo-hell. I'd lost my soul and couldn't get release for judgement.

Years later after, they planted Lester, we were able to 'commiserate' together. We were father and son, bound by a Demon from Satan." He became quiet again.

I sat in wonder, at this man's tale. What a sad life for him and his son, Lester. I looked up into his hooded eyes, and ask. "What do you have to do to be released, and get on with…. what ever it is, you'll be getting on with?"

He gave me a long dark look and leaned forward, putting his withered hand on my shoulder. "The Devil-woman must be broken, defeated, and banished back to the depths of Hell! She has tormented many souls like ours over the millenniums. She never dies, and continues on to this day!"

"What's perdition, or Hell like?" I asked.

He smiled and leaned back in the rocker. "You're lookin at it son. Actual Hell is knowin' that Heaven is so close, so close, that you can see it, smell it, feel it, but to be locked out! That is true 'Hell' my boy. There are many of us trapped like this because of one Bitch! Your the one boy. The one, that can make things right!"

A cool breeze seemed to make my flesh tingle, as I asked, "What can I do?"

"Son, you need to reach down deep into your Christian soul. Down deep, where it counts. Find all the inner strength God gave you, and summon it. Now, stand and come closer." As I stood, Lester appeared out of the mist by the Old man's side. They both reached to me and beckoned, with outstretched hands. I went closer and we embraced. The old man never rising, Lester and I, bending over him. Both, let their hands go up to the back of my head.

I smiled knowingly, and said, " Now I understand. I have the mark also. I learned of the knot's mystery long ago, and some of our dark heritage. I have encountered some tough times, but have been blessed with a wonderful family and home. Now, I am also afraid of what's next."

The embrace ended, Lester and I stood. With his hand on my shoulder, he smiled and looked me in the eye, "We now understand each other. Same background, same luck, same un.. unner…"

"Unreliability's!" Interjected the old man. "Many of your

forebearers have fallen, just as Lester and I have. We gave up our souls, to lust! We were embarrassed either publicly, like Lester, or privately, like my own sorry ending."

Lester was fervently nodding, and blurted "Like your fath…..uh oh!"

I now, knew the rest. I cringed at the memory. My father had been of low birth, but through hard work and extraordinary luck, had 'it all' at one time. A prosperous farm, fine family and plenty of money. He lost it all. Tears filled my eyes as I stood before these two apparitions. They seemed to read my thoughts.

The old man rose from the chair. "Had it all didn't he? Went down into the bottle, and lost every thing. Died a transient bum." He put his hand on my arm. "It's okay, it's okay."

I cried outloud, remembering the anger and hate I'd felt when he'd abandoned us. Never wanting to see him, but longing for him at the same time! The unrequited love was a tremendous burden on my soul. It nearly took my mind at one time, but I'd fought back, determined more than ever to have a whole and complete life, and make my family 'solid.'

I dried my eyes on my sleeve and looked at the two, who stood silently watching. "Then he…….?!

"Yes," said Lester, "He came to fall under de spell of de witch woman, too."

"Some of us go quickly, afterwards," said Isaac, "Some of us die slowly. A thousand tormented deaths, like your father." After a silent pause Isaac again took my hand, and said, "He loved you."

I was spent. I sat on the cool grass with my head cradled in my arms. No more tears would come, only relief and forgiveness. I looked up at them after a bit and asked, "Where is my father?"

Isaac waved his arm, "Oh he's out there. Lord knows where, but in the same condition as us. No use for you to worry 'bout tryin' to find him. Best way is for you to get ready, inside yourself. Go and prepare your own soul. Then maybe you can help all your kinfolk."

I had a thought, tilted my head, and looked carefully at the two of them. "Isaac, are we related?"

Lester grinned and said "He catch on real quick, fo' a dumb white boy. Don't he?"

"Behave yerself, boy!" Isaac admonished. "Yes, he admitted. All of us with the mark, share the same strange and mysterious heritage, lost in the pages of history. Your great, great, grandfather was my twin brother. He also survived the massacre, but was taken in by another family. We were raised just a few miles apart, but never told. Families were already large, and could only take in so many. Both families, and all that knew, felt it better that way."

"The Retherford's?" I asked.

"Correct." Said a smiling Isaac. "You do know, some of your heritage then!"

"Charles Retherford," I related, "The only survivor of an Indian massacre. Taken in by the Retherfords. Grew to manhood, and married 'Nancy.' Had eight children, but disappeared in 1851, while out hunting. After an appropriate period, Nancy went across the hollow and married the old bachelor, Jesse Grimes. He adopted the children. Hence, my great grandfather, Charles Grimes.

He had a good life, until an encounter on the road to his cabin, led to the killing of a man. He, and his family, fled the mountains and came north. My grandfather, Charles' son, eventually worked his way up to Indiana with his family, and here I am! Correct?"

"Pretty much so." said Lester, "Course, de Devil witch played a fair sized part, in all those strange happenin's." Isaac nodded in agreement.

I nodded, "My grandpa fathered twelve children, but they scattered all over the Nation."

Lester laughed and said. "Yes ol Gilbert was a 'vigorous man', an' he sired a lot more den......."

"Shut up Lester!" a stern-faced Isaac said. "The boy don't need the whole danged mess on his mind, right now." He turned to me, "Son, your grandpappy was a good man, but he never had the mark. Must've skipped a generation, but it came back 'with a vengeance' on your daddy."

"I know." I hung my head in shame for the feelings I'd had against the man all these years. I looked at Isaac. "What about me? I've been successful and happy, these last years. I must be getting close to my 'destiny of destruction.' What can I do?"

"Once again, I tell you boy, keep your faith, and seek strength in God. Of all the lineage of us, you are the one who has faithfully been connected with God. Even when you were going through those terrible years, you still were in the 'churchhouse.'

I shook my head "I'm no saint! It's true I've always been in the church, but there have been many times when I strayed, and struggled with my religion. There were times of non-belief, and ridicule of God. I've sinned more then you know!"

"Yes son, we know." said Isaac, "But you never gave up the faith, totally. You've strayed, it's true but unlike us, you've always returned to your faith, and begged God for forgiveness. He is a father. You are a son. Fathers will always love their sons and be willing to forgive. Just let it happen. Your guilt and troubles are like a sack of rocks, son. Just lay it down, and go on, unburdened."

He was right. I had committed my share of misdeeds and excesses, but I also saw the little boy in the second hand sports coat, out by the gravel road at the end of the lane, in the 1950's. He was waiting for the neighbors to pick him up, for the ride to church and Sunday school. For some reason, God always pulled at me, and for some reason, I'd responded. I closed my eyes, and saw my life before me. All the events, both good and bad, leading up to this day. I began to wonder, was I a true person, or just and actor in a play, readying for the final scene?

"Hey," said Lester, "Don' you be haven no bad thoughts 'bout youself. You stay by de Lord and keep de faith. He protect and guide you. You be de life-force fo' all us. Be ready fo de dark Bitch, son, she test yo faith and pull you to her, 'iffin you weaken. Keep yo' head wif God!"

"He's right son." said Isaac," We're finished here. Our job is complete. Now it's on your shoulders. Sorry to burden you so, but you have more goin' for you than we ever did." They both embraced me, and with tears in their pleading eyes, turned and walked into the mist.

"No wait!" I cried. "I have so many questions. What happens now?"

I saw them no longer, but a voice from the fog whispered….. "Trust in the Lord."

I awoke from a 'trancelike' state, on my knees by the grave of the old soldier. No 'real time' seemed to have past, though I was exhausted. It was twilight. I rose, and began a slow and weary walk, towards home.

# Chapter 16

For the next few days, I lived in a fog of fear, despair, and wonder. It was all too much to comprehend and believe. I had not one 'physical thread' of proof, that the incidents actually happened. For all I knew, they were a series of strokes, or broken blood vessels in my head. I had no physical after-affects, but anything is possible.

As time went by, and nothing happened, I began to function 'normally' again. I went to school, and enjoyed my classes as usual. Took my afternoon walks, although not, through the graveyard as often. When I did go, the cemetery was quiet and peaceful. As I stood by the grave of Isaac and Lester, nothing happened, even when I called to them.

I resumed my weekend walks in the woods around our home. I began to enjoy the countryside, without looking over my shoulder and cringing at every creak of a limb in the breeze.

The winter came and went, uneventfully. The only excitement came when all the kids were home at Christmas, and a terrible snowstorm hit. Our steep driveway, that is nine-hundred feet in length, became a frozen sled run. We had a car, and a truck, off the side at the same time. Had to use my old Ford tractor to pull them out. No injuries or damages. We all hunkered down, by the family room stove when the electricity went off. Later, by the 'majestic' greatroom fireplace, as the snow fell. The snowstorm was a winter 'wonderland' performance, before our all-windowed, south wall.

My two oldest, twenty-four year old twins, were out of college and employed. Aaron, was a Park ranger, in a National park in the far north region of Indiana. Heather, was employed as an Occupational Therapist at a rehab hospital in Indy. Megan, was a Sophomore in College, majoring in nursing. Kelsey, was a Junior in high school. Jenni, was happily teaching the third graders, at the local school. All was well, as we gathered for the Christmas Eve candlelight service at our church. I gave thanks for all my blessings, and prayed to God to deliver us, from the depths of this snowy winter safely.

It was good to be wrapped in the 'family womb.' I spent hours by the fire, enjoying the panoramic view of the Whitewater Valley. I could just see, past the old middle school, into the graveyard with its' snow covered tombstones. I often contemplated the meaning of my life. I wondered if God had sent the message as a dream, as a sign, that I should rethink my bad thoughts about my father, and forgive. Maybe, that was the purpose of it all. Living with anger and guilt is a terrible burden. I decided to try and put down that 'sack of rocks,'… and go on.

As I said, the winter passed. The kids went their ways, and Jenni and I 'plowed along,' with our careers. Spring came, and the school year ended. It was a summer of fun and pleasure for me. I worked my properties and tended my cattle. Evenings were spent sitting in the doorway of my barn, which overlooked the nearby neighborhood. Friends came by, we swapped stories, and told some whoppers. It was "Mayberry" all over. I actually began to forget the 'traumatic visitations' of the previous autumn. Then, the next Autumn came.

I normally enjoy the autumn seasons. The smell of burning leaves, and the slight change to cooler breezes, refresh us. It brings with it a warning, to enjoy the final vestiges of summer warmth, before the raging, but beautiful winter weather moves in.

This Autumn was different. I felt a sense of unease, deep in my being. As I walked the woods, gloom would often pervade my soul. I quickly headed for the sunlight. It was like an itch that I couldn't quite scratch.

That early October, I walked into the cemetery again. It was a Monday. I'd spent a contented weekend of work on my small farm, a few miles west of the town. Sunday evening, I prepared for the week of classes, and was ready for the kids. Monday was a nice day and I'd enjoyed the classes. Had fun and laughter, and abit of learning.

After school, I'd fed my four heifers and calves, changed into comfortable walking clothes, and headed out for the evening walk. Out of curiosity, I wondered into the cemetery. It was very peaceful and quiet. I felt nothing, but called out, "I'm here! Where are you?" I called aloud again, "I need you! Please come to me!" Behind me, I heard the creak of a rocker, and quickly turned to see an elderly couple staring at me, from their chairs on their front porch across the street. "Oh crap!" I said to myself, "Now everyone will think I'm batty." I waved. They stared. I walked out of the graveyard and into the street, and called to them.

"A rough day! Classes were bad and I 'had it out' with the wife! Just venting a bit, to God!" I sheepishly walked by the

Anderson's porch. Mr. Anderson leaned forward and quietly said, "We'll pray for you, and yours."

"Thanks." I waved and shuffled on towards home. Well, I could use the prayers.

As the days, weeks, and months rolled by, I tried to talk to my wife and children about our heritage, and the strange goings-on, but was met with looks of apprehension and doubt. I turned inward to my diary, and wrote of my experiences and my fears. I even began to write, in 'story form', about the strange happenings. This was a 'cover,' to use with the family. I told them it was all material I'd dreamed up, and intended to use.

I was able to lose myself in my writings, and actually confront my doubts, and innermost fears. More and more, I delved into my religious background. I spoke with my minister, and resolved questions in my mind that I'd pondered for a lifetime. Things were getting back to normal. Life was good.

As the years passed by, I became a father-in-law and a grandfather, three times. I felt immortalized through my children and grandchildren. Life was a joy, and I thanked my God daily for the blessings he rained down upon me.

I became a leader of the church, and a 'pillar' of the community. I was involved in many charitable organizations, and a tireless worker for the needy. The need to give and help was a passion and a satisfaction for me, an atonement for past sins, and possible future trials.

I began to write a story. It was a tale of tormented men, of Isaac and Lester. I worked on the writings each evening, and basically, retold what they had shared with me in years past. I tried to share some of the stories with my wife, but she dismissed them with a strange look and said, "Are you alright. You seem to be going through a change, lately." I talked to my children about my 'story.' They too, thought it was a bit weird. I gave up.

The writing continued slowly, until I came to the end of my dealings with Lester and Isaac. I could not think of a proper ending. I let the unfinished work lay. I believed the ending would come to me someday. I hoped to be around to write it…..Then, the ending came.

# Chapter 17

It was a sunny, autumn day. I had my trusty walking stick in hand, and was making my rounds, through the wooded area in the valley below my home. It was in the area where old Isaac had built his cabin. There was the indentation of his rock-lined well, and a few stones, of what must have been part of the foundation to his home. I discovered it many years ago, and put things together in my mind. I was at first, afraid to go there, but as time passed, I went to the area often. I liked to reflect on the early settler, and what it must have been like, to live in those 'bygone times.'

I walked a bit more slowly these days. Now, in my late 'fifties', my hip bothered me more and more. I had a limp, from an accident with an angry bull, and the leg bothered me when the weather was changing. The limp was more pronounced with each passing year. The walking stick was a necessity, rather than a conversation piece.

It was great to be out in the cool evening air. The fragrance of the woods filled me with vigor. I could hear the sounds of my hometown, three-quarters of a mile to the south. Birds chirped and squirrels barked and scolded from the treetops….. Then,…. all was silent.

My first thought, was that my ears had plugged. I shook my head and tapped my hand against it. Nothing. I was seeing very clearly, but no sounds! Had I lost my hearing?

A voice, came through the silence.

"No, you be jus fine my boy." she said. A shiver went through my body. I knew my time had come. I slowly turned around, my neck hairs prickling, and faced the beautiful, young, dark-skinned girl.

She was a beauty! Her wicked smile, promised hidden mysteries. I swallowed, and spoke, "You finally came for me." Anger and hatred filled my mind. "Why did you wait so long? I've expected you for many years."

She laughed quietly, and stood with her head held high, arms bent, her hands on her hips. "Wanted you to enjoy life, an taste the fruits of you labors. Have been very lucky, dat right?"… I nodded.

"Wanted you to be ready fo' me. Come now boy! Time to pay de piper." She extended her arms, hands motioning me to come. "Come, come taste my 'sweets' boy! You be immortal. Do yo' duty to de master!"

"Jesus save me!" I cried, and dropped to my knees, in prayer.

She laughed again. "Jesus, got nuttin to be doin' wit dis boy! Forget your 'pie in de sky.' Have in here, and now!" She ripped of her blouse and skirt, and stood naked before me, glistening with sweat. I could smell her musky scent. My body reacted.

I fought with temptation, the vision of Isaac and Lester came before me. I could feel their torment. I concentrated on images of my wife and children. I screamed, "No! Go back to Hell, you bitch! Tell him you failed with this one!" I grabbed the gold crucifix from around my neck, and thrust it at her.

She threw back her head and gave an unearthly roar. "Ha, Ha! Boy you seen to many silly movies!" She reached out, and took the cross in her hand. It sizzled and melted. She rubbed the molten metal over her body, and thrust her bare pelvis forward. "Look, into your past! See, into your future!"

As I felt myself being pulled to her! I strained to hold back. I was shaking and drenched with perspiration. My fists clenched, my muscles were taunt. The force was unstoppable! Then,…. I heard the dogs.The sounds of ferocious barking, were coming from south of the clearing. The roars of my two boxers, 'Jake and Sam,' were unmistakable to my ears. With a start, the 'banshee' turned to look. I made a quick grab at the walking stick, I'd dropped earlier. She turned back, just as I thrust it to her breast.

The stick broke, but entered just under the ribcage! Her forward momentum pushed it up, and in! She jerked backwards! She stood erect with her back arched and head tilted skyward. As dark blood spurted from the horrible wound, she screamed a wild cry, unto the skies. She staggered back, grabbed at the broken lance, and pulled it from her chest. Blood gushed! She dropped to her knees, and hung her head. As her lifeblood poured out, she slowly raised her eyes to me. Blood, was on her lips, as she said, "You have ruint it! You bastard-son! Done broken de link! A curse be on you!"

I stood over her, and said, "Dam you, to Eternal Hell, you heathen Bitch! You've cursed me, and my kinfolk, for all this time. One more won't hurt!"

She rolled to her back, as the dogs entered the clearing. "I be back for you boy! Dis not over!"

It was my turn to laugh, and quietly say, "This time, it is over, woman. I'll be ready, and prepared, if you ever want to try again. I gave my soul to God, many years ago. Fight him, for it!"

She gave a long moaning cry, and the dogs were upon her. They tried to bite her flesh, but quickly backed off, as she flailed at them. Then, shevanished, in a puff of smoke. The dogs tilted their heads, and stood looking at the scene, bewildered. My son, Aaron, walked into the clearing.

He saw the smoke, the clothes, the blood on the ground, and me. He ran to me, we embraced. Tears rolled down my cheeks as he explained, "Dad, I'm sorry I doubted you." He said. "We've worried so long. Mom called me, she was very upset. I came as soon as I could. She'd read some of your diaries and showed them to me. We didn't understand!" He too, had tears.

I held him at arms length. "Son, I'm not sure I understand it all, myself. I just know it's over. She's gone. She could overcome anything except the love of God and family. I feel free, at last!" We held each other, for what seemed a long time.

When we finally broke the embrace, he gave me a knowing look, nodded his head, and said, "Thanks dad." With arms over each others' shoulders, we slowly walked out of the clearing and towards home.

# Chapter 18

As we came up the hill to the house, I heard laughter and talking. As we rounded the bend, I saw several people on the upper and lower decks, milling about in a festive mood. My wife, Jenni, met us at the front steps. She was smiling. "I don't know what's happened." she said. "I felt the urge to cook and bake. No sooner had I began, when all these strange men showed up, from nowhere. It's funny, but I felt comfortable with them being here, almost like I should know them. It seems like a holiday."

I looked up at the staring faces, and said,… "I think, I do know them."

I walked up the steps and across the deck. Several older fellows, dressed in clothing of times past, shook my hand and patted my shoulder. Pleasantries were exchanged, all round. I saw Isaac and Lester coming towards me. We stood together, and smiled, with arms around each other.

Lester, grinned and said, "Well, you done it boy! Beat dat woman. We get our chance at redemption at last!"

Isaac gave my shoulder a squeeze, and said, "Yes, we knowed you were the one, son. Yer faith in God and strong family love won out. You've done well with your family. The girls, are on their way here now, although they don't know why. They just know you need them." We looked at each other in silence. He spoke again, "Yes, all these folks are kin, both close and distant. They all came, with special permission, so's they could thank you." Everyone nodded, a few friendly words were spoken. "Now, we don't have much time, but there's someone here you should meet." He turned and the crowd parted.

A young man with dark, wavy hair and a dark complexion, was sitting in a chair at the end of the deck. He wore worn kakhi pants, and a faded denim shirt, his old wristwatch, hanging from the button hole in the collar. He smiled and stood….. It was my father.

Isaac and Lester pushed me gently, towards him. "Dad?" I tentatively ask, "Dad?" I knew. He greeted me with open arms. As we hugged, I could smell the smells of long ago, his sweat and his strength, as we rode the old 'John Deere' tractor, through the 'fields of my boyhood.'

"Son, I'm sorry for the pain." He said, as he held me, "I..I…

"Its alright, Dad. I understand," No further words needed be said. We all understood.

There was a coughing, and clearing of many throats as we broke the long embrace. I nodded my head and smiled at them all.

"No there's not time for introductions, Son." said Isaac. "We're all kin, some close, some distant. All share the same story. Just wanted to say thanks, and get on to final judgement."

"Final judgement?" I ask, "What if it doesn't go, as you hoped?"

"Oh, said my father, "We're willing to accept any fate, as

may be. We know that we'll be judged, as mortal men, who were playing against a 'stacked deck.' Hopefully, Saint Peter will have those gates held open for the lot of us. If not, at least we had the chance. Purgatory, is hell! We've already been there." He stepped to me and placed his hands on my shoulders. "Its because of you son. Thank you." There was a chorus of huzzahs, and more words of gratitude. The men began to file down the steps and head off towards the woods. The four of us, Lester, Isaac, my father, and I stood together.

Lester spoke. "We be leavin' too boy. We be seein' you again, someday. Jus', you take yur sweet time." I, once again, hugged each of them. Tears flowed freely. My father was the last.

He whispered, "Live a good long life son! I'm living through you, also. Be the man I tried, and failed, to be." I couldn't speak. I nodded.

He walked down the steps, across the yard, and turned before he entered the trees. My father called out, "I'm proud of you! I always loved you, and always will!" With a final goodbye wave, he was gone.

My wife and son came up beside me. I put an arm around Jen's waist. Aaron, placed his arm on my shoulder. In the twilight, we saw the headlights of three cars coming up the drive. My daughters and their families.

I could now write the ending to my story.

The End

*Dedicated to my father,*
*Charles Edward Grimes.*
*He had great luck, both good and bad.*
*Dad, I understand and I forgive.*
*2/16/02*